9
SUGAR CREEK GANG
ONE STORMY DAY

Paul Hutchens

MOODY PRESS
CHICAGO

PREFACE

Hi—from a member of the Sugar Creek Gang!

It's just that I don't know which one I am. When I was good, I was Little Jim. When I did bad things—well, sometimes I was Bill Collins or even mischievous Poetry.

You see, I am the daughter of Paul Hutchens, and I spent many an hour listening to him read his manuscript as far as he had written it that particular day. I went along to the north woods of Minnesota, to Colorado, and to the various other places he would go to find something different for the Gang to do.

Now the years have passed—more than fifty, actually. My father is in heaven, but the Gang goes on. All thirty-six books are still in print and now are being updated for today's readers with input from my five children, who also span the decades from the '50s to the '70s.

The real Sugar Creek is in Indiana, and my father and his six brothers were the original Gang. But the idea of the books and their ministry were and are the Lord's. It is He who keeps the Gang going.

PAULINE HUTCHENS WILSON

1

The trouble the Sugar Creek Gang had with our new teacher started the very first day we started to school again after Christmas vacation. As you maybe know, we all had flown down to Palm Tree Island and came back to find that, while we were gone, our pretty lady teacher had gotten married and had resigned from being teacher. We were going to have a *man* teacher instead to finish out the year. Imagine that! A *man* teacher for the Sugar Creek School, when all we'd ever had had been *lady* teachers whom we'd all liked. We were all plenty mad. Plenty!

We might not have had all the trouble, though, if it hadn't been for Shorty Long, the new tough guy who had moved into the neighborhood and who was just starting at our school.

As I said, the trouble started the very first day. Just before eight o'clock that morning, I was flying around in our house like a chicken with its head off, looking for my cap and mittens and asking Mom if my lunch box was ready. Mom was trying to keep Charlotte Ann, my baby sister, quiet so she and I could hear each other; Dad was in the living room trying to listen to the morning news on the radio; and

Poetry, the barrel-shaped member of our gang, was out by the big walnut tree near our front gate, whistling and yelling for me to hurry up or we'd be late; and I couldn't find my arithmetic book—which are all the reasons that I wasn't in a very good humor to start off to school.

So it was the easiest thing in the world for me to get mad quick, when, about ten or maybe fifteen minutes later, we met Shorty Long, the new tough guy who'd moved into our neighborhood, down at the end of the lane.

Anyway, pretty soon I was out of our house, slamming the door after me and dashing out through the snow path I'd shoveled that morning myself, toward Poetry, who was at the gate, waiting.

I wasn't any farther than twenty noisy steps away from the house when I heard the kitchen door open behind me, and my dad's big voice thundered out after me and said, *"Jasper!"* which is my middle name and which I don't like. My whole name is William Jasper Collins, but I'd rather be called just plain "Bill," because that is what the gang calls me. And besides, Dad never called me Jasper except when I had done something wrong or he thought I had. So when he thundered after me, *"Jasper!"* I stopped dead in my tracks and looked back.

Dad's big bushy, reddish-blackish eyebrows were down, and his jaw was hard-looking, and I knew right away I'd done something wrong.

"What?" I called back to him, starting toward the gate again. "I've got to hurry, or I'll be late."

"Come back and shut the door *decently!*" Dad said, and when he says things like that to me *like* that, I nearly always obey him quick or wish I had.

I was halfway back to the door when Poetry squawked from the gate, saying, "Hurry up, Bill!" which I did.

I dashed back to our kitchen door and had started to shut it decently, when Dad stopped me and said, "Remember now, Son, you boys behave yourselves today. Mr. Black is a fine man, and you'll like him all right just as soon as you get used to him!"

"We won't," I said. I'd already made up my mind I *wasn't* going to like him because he was a *man* teacher, because we'd never had a man at Sugar Creek School, and also because we had all liked our pretty lady teacher so well that we didn't want anybody else!

"What do you mean, you *won't?*" Dad said, still holding the door open so that I couldn't shut it decently. "You mean you won't behave yourselves?"

"I'll be *late!*" I said. "I've got to go—Poetry's *waiting* for me!"

My dad raised his voice all of a sudden and yelled to Poetry, "Hold your horses, Leslie Thompson"—which is Poetry's real name. "The first bell hasn't rung yet!"

And it hadn't. When it *did* ring, there

would still be a half hour for us to get to school, which didn't start until half past eight.

But we all liked to get there early on a Monday morning, though, so that we could see each other, none of us having seen all of us for two or three days. We might meet some of the gang on the way—Circus, our acrobat; Big Jim, our leader; Little Jim, the best Christian in the gang; pop-eyed Dragonfly; and maybe Little Tom Till, the new member. Tom's big brother, Bob, had caused us a lot of trouble last year, but he'd quit school and had gone away to a city and was working in a factory.

You know, about every year we had some new boy move into our neighborhood, and nearly always we had trouble with him until he found out whether he was going to get to run the gang or was just going to *try* to, and always it turned out that he only *tried* to. Also, we always had to decide whether the new guy was going to be a member of the gang—and sometimes he couldn't be.

"Jasper Collins!" my dad said to me, still holding our back door open so that I couldn't shut it decently—and also holding onto my collar with his other hand—"you're not going another inch until you promise me you'll treat Mr. Black decently. Promise me that!"

Just that second my mom's voice called from some part of our house and said, "For land's sake, shut the door! We can't heat up the whole farm!"

"I can't!" I yelled back to her. "Dad won't let me!"

Well, that certainly didn't make my dad feel very good, and I shouldn't have said it, because it was being sarcastic. Anyway, Dad tightened his grip on my collar and kind of jerked me back and said to me under his breath so that Poetry wouldn't hear, "We'll settle this tonight when you get home."

"Can I go now, then?" I said.

And he said, "Yes"—still under his breath—"I can't very well correct you while Poetry is here." And that is one reason I liked my parents —they never gave me a hard calling down when we had company but always waited till later.

The very second my dad let me loose, I shot away from our back door like a rock shooting out of a boy's sling, straight for Poetry and the front gate. I got to where Poetry was holding the gate open for me just as I heard my dad shut our back door decently.

Poetry and I were already talking and listening to each other and being terribly glad to be together again, when our kitchen door opened again and Dad's big voice thundered after me, *"Bill!"*

"What?" I yelled, and he yelled back to me, "Shut that *gate!*" which I ran back and did without saying anything.

A jiffy later Poetry and I were swishing through the snow toward Sugar Creek School—not knowing it was the beginning of a very exciting day and also the beginning of a lot of new trouble for the Sugar Creek Gang.

We were *ker-squashing* along through the snow, making our own path with our feet—there hadn't been any cars or sleighs on our road yet that morning because ours wasn't an arterial road—when Poetry said all of a sudden, "My pop says we've got to like the new teacher."

"My dad told me the same thing," I said and sighed, knowing it was going to be hard to like somebody I already didn't like.

Well, we soon came to the north road, where we saw, coming across the Sugar Creek bridge, two boys and a lot of girls. Right away I knew the girls were Circus's sisters. One of them was named Lucille and was maybe the nicest girl in all of Sugar Creek School and was just my age, and she wasn't afraid of spiders and mice and things, and sometimes she smiled at me across the schoolroom. And walking right beside Lucille on the other side of Circus was another guy, and it was Shorty Long, the new boy who'd moved into our neighborhood and whom I didn't like!

"Look!" Poetry said to me. "Shorty Long is carrying two lunch boxes!"

"He's big enough to *need* two," I said and didn't like him even worse.

"Looks like it's Lucille's lunch box," Poetry said, and the very minute he said it I knew what he meant . . .

Almost right away I wondered if there was

maybe going to be another fight between Shorty Long and me—I'd had a fierce one just before the Sugar Creek Gang had flown down to Palm Tree Island.

Well, Shorty Long raised his voice and yelled to us something in that crazy new language he'd started us all to talking, which Dragonfly liked so well, and which is called "Openglopish"—which you talk by just putting an "op" in front of all the vowel sounds in your words.

So this is what Shorty Long yelled to us: "Hopi, Bopill! Hopi, Popo-opetropy!"—which is Openglopish for "Hi, Bill! Hi, Poetry!"

I really think I would have liked the language if Shorty Long hadn't been the one to start it in the Sugar Creek neighborhood.

Before I knew what I was going to say, I said, looking at Lucille's red lunch box in Shorty Long's left hand, "Keep still. Talk English! Don't call me 'Bopill'! Take that other syllable off!"

Even as far away as I was, I thought I saw his red face turn redder, and then he yelled to me and said, "All right, if you don't want to be a good sport, I'll take it off. From now on you're just plain 'Pill.' *Pill* as in *caterpillar.*"

And that started the fuse on my fiery temper to burning very fast. I saw red, and Lucille's red lunch box didn't help any. Besides, I was already mad from having all that trouble with my dad. Besides that, also I'd always carried Lucille's lunch box myself when Big Jim was along and he carried our new minister's daughter's lunch box at the same time.

In fact, it was Big Jim's being especially polite to Sylvia, our minister's daughter, that got me started being kind to a girl myself—girls belonging to the human race, also.

"I'll carry your box for you," I said to Circus's sister and started to reach for it.

But Shorty Long interrupted my hand and said loftily, "Don't disturb the lady!" Then he swung around quick and shoved me terribly hard with his shoulder and walked on beside Lucille.

At the same minute, my boots got tangled up in each other, and I found myself going down a deep ditch backward and sideways and headfirst all at the same time into a big snowdrift—which was the beginning of the fight.

Just as I was trying to untangle myself from myself and struggle to my feet, I heard a couple of yells coming from different directions. I looked up to see Little Jim and Dragonfly running across from the woods. And at the same time, I also heard a girl's fierce voice saying, "*You* can't carry my lunch box! I'll carry it myself!"

I looked up from my snowdrift just in time to see Shorty Long whirl around with the red lunch box in his hand and hold it out so that Circus's sister couldn't reach it. I also looked just in time to see a pair of flying feet, which looked like Dragonfly's, make a dive for Shorty Long, and then there were three of us in that big snowdrift at the same time. Also at the same time, I heard a lunch box go *squash* with the sound of a glass and maybe a spoon or a fork or something inside, and that was that.

Well, all I had to do was to turn over on my stomach, and I was on top of Shorty Long. And being mad, I felt as strong as the village blacksmith whose "muscles on his brawny arms were strong as iron bands." So I yelled and grunted to Shorty Long between short pants of breath, "You will forget to wash your face in the morning, will you! Doesn't your mother teach you to wash your face before you go to school? Shame on you!" All of a sudden I remembered I'd forgotten to wash mine.

Right away I was scooping up handfuls of snow and washing Shorty's Long's face and neck and saying to him, "I'll teach you to throw an innocent girl's lunch box around like that."

Boy, oh, boy, I tell you, I felt fine on top of Shorty Long, imagining how everybody up on the road was watching and feeling proud of me. Even Circus's sister would be proud of me, a *little* guy licking the stuffings out of a great big lummox like Shorty Long! Why, I was hardly half as big as he was, and I was licking him in a fight right in front of everybody! It felt good!

Just that minute the school bell rang, and I knew we all ought to get going if we wanted to get to school ahead of time and sort of look at the teacher, and maybe I ought to clean out my desk a little too, not having done it the day before our Christmas vacation had begun.

So I jerked myself loose from Shorty Long, scrambled to my feet, shook my cap, knocked off some of the snow, and climbed back up into the road again, where I thought everybody had been standing watching the fight. I guess maybe I really expected them to say something about the wonderful fight I'd won, but would you believe it? The girls and Poetry had walked on up the road. I looked for the red lunch box and also for mine. But the red one wasn't any-where around. Then I saw it, swinging back and forth in Circus's sister's hand, about fifty feet up the road.

"I'll carry it for you," I said when I caught up with the rest of the crowd.

And would you believe *this*? It was the most disgusting thing that ever happened, and it made me mad all over the inside of me. That girl I'd made a fool out of myself to be a hero for didn't even appreciate all I'd done, not even the fact that I'd given some of my life's blood for her (which I had, for my nose was bleeding a little, and for the first time I noticed my jaw hurt too, where Shorty Long must have hit me).

She looked at me as if I was so much chaff blowing out of a threshing machine and said, "Can't you live one day without getting into a fight? I think Shorty Long is nice."

Well, that spoiled my day. In fact, it looked as if it had spoiled my whole life maybe.

"All right, Smarty," I said, "you can work your own arithmetic problems this year."

And I walked behind them and on the other side of the road all the rest of the way to our red brick schoolhouse, which with its two front windows and its one door between them, and the little roofless porch, looked sort of like a red-faced boy's face, with a scowl on it.

"'S'matter?" I heard somebody say beside me, and it was Little Jim, swishing along, carrying his stick in one hand and his own lunch box in the other.

"Nothing," I said, but I felt better right away. Little Jim could do that to a guy—make him feel better just by asking, "'S'matter?" which he always did when I was bothered about something.

"Dad says we have to *like* Mr. Black, the new teacher," Little Jim said and struck hard at a chokecherry shrub that was growing close to the road, knocking snow off of it. Some of the cold snow hit me in the hot face and felt good.

I didn't say anything. Little Jim's mentioning his dad made me think of mine, and I remembered that he'd said, "We'll settle it tonight," so I kept on walking along, not saying anything else—not even wanting to say anything else and knowing my whole day was ruined.

The next thing Little Jim said didn't help me feel any better, either. He said, "We found out last night that Shorty Long's first name is 'William.'"

He struck at another chokecherry shrub, which scattered some more snow in my face, and I said, "*What*? Why—that's my first name! How'd you find out? Who told you?"

"*His* mom told *my* mom," Little Jim said. "She went to church with us last night, you know."

I'd seen Mrs. Long last night while she sat in our little church with the Foote family— Little Jim's last name is Foote. As you know, Little Jim's mom is the pianist in our church and is maybe the best player in all Sugar Creek territory. Also Little Jim's parents are always looking for somebody to take to church and are what my dad calls "soul winners"—that is, they are always trying to get somebody to become Christians.

"Mom wants to get Shorty Long's mom saved," Little Jim said.

He was socking every chokecherry shrub we came to, and I was getting madder and madder at Shorty Long for spoiling my whole day. Also I was holding my nose tight with my handkerchief to help it stop bleeding.

"Is Shorty Long's *pop* saved?" I asked.

Little Jim socked a tall snow-covered mullein stalk with his stick, knocking off the snow and some brown seeds at the same time, so hard that what he said came out of his small mouth as if he had thrown his words at me very hard. "Nope! And he's mad at some of the Sugar Creek Gang for being mean to his boy. He's told our new teacher we're a gang of roughnecks and to look out for us!"

"Did Shorty Long's mom tell your mom that?" I asked.

Little Jim said, "Yep, last night in our car—"

Then Little Jim stopped with his stick in the air and looked over and up at me and sort of whispered, "Shorty Long won't go to church because his pop won't. Maybe his parents'll get a divorce, Mom said, if they don't get saved first."

"A divorce?" I said. "What for?"

"'Cause William's pop is too mean, and swears so much at his mom, and doesn't want her to go to church."

I could hear Dragonfly and Shorty Long talking behind me. They were talking that crazy Openglopish language, just chattering back and forth as if they were the very best of friends.

"But they don't call him *Bill*," Little Jim said, talking again about Shorty Long's first name. "They call him *William*."

All this time Dragonfly and Shorty Long were getting closer and closer behind us, and I could hear the crazy words they were tossing back and forth to each other like two boys throwing softballs.

Just that minute Shorty Long said in Openglopish, "Mopistoper Blopack opis gropeat. OpI'll bopet hope gopives Bopill Copollopins opa dopetopentopiopon topodopay." And I knew exactly what he had said. It was "Mr. Black is great. I'll bet he gives Bill Collins a detention today."

I pressed my lips together tight and kept still, making up my mind at the same time that I *wasn't* going to get any detention.

We all hurried on toward the schoolhouse. The minute I got there I went straight to the iron pump near the big maple tree and put cold water on my face and nose, washing off some of the good red blood I'd shed for a worthless girl. The cold water helped to make my nose stop bleeding. I also rinsed out my handkerchief, being especially glad Mom had made me take two with me, which she nearly always does in the wintertime just in case I catch a cold or something, which I sometimes do.

While I was washing my face, Poetry came over and watched me and said, "You certainly licked the stuffings out of William Long."

"Thanks," I said. "But what'd they ever give him that crazy name for?"

And before the day was over, I wished that *my* name hadn't been William, either. In fact, before the morning had hardly gotten started, I was into trouble with Mr. Black. And it all happened on account of Shorty Long and I having the same first name. I even hate to tell you what happened, but it's all a part of the story. So here goes.

First thing, though, before school took up we all got together in the school woodshed and held a special gang meeting. I told the gang what Little Jim told me that his mom said Shorty Long's mom said about what Shorty Long's mean pop told Mr. Black about the Sugar Creek Gang being a bunch of roughnecks.

Then we all voted that we wouldn't *be* that.

We were going to prove to our new teacher that we weren't.

Just before the last bell rang, Big Jim gave us all orders to behave ourselves and said, "If any of us doesn't behave, he'll have to be called in and stand trial by the rest of us."

Then the bell rang, and in we went.

2

It's a crazy feeling, coming back to school after a super Christmas vacation and having a new teacher, a *man* teacher with shell-rimmed glasses and a head that is bald in the middle, and who has one all-gold tooth right in front. Seeing that gold tooth made me think of Dragonfly, whose large front teeth were much too large for his very small face.

School had been going on for a while, and it was maybe after eleven o'clock, and the first grade was up on the long bench in front of Mr. Black's desk, with different ones in the first grade standing whenever Mr. Black told them to and coming to stand beside him, where he sat at his big desk, and reading out loud, making it hard for the rest of us to study, which it always is in a one-room school anyway.

I looked across the schoolroom to Dragonfly, who was next to the wall beside the front window, and he happened to be looking at me at the same time. He had a mischievous grin on his always mischievous face, and just as I looked he folded a little piece of paper and slipped it across the aisle to Poetry, who slipped it across another aisle to Circus, who slipped it across to me.

Mr. Black was very busy, and I had already

made up my mind that because the lenses of his glasses were very thick, he probably couldn't see back in the schoolroom very far but could see better while he was reading.

I was supposed to be studying geography at the time, and I had my big geography book standing up on my desk in front of me. It was the easiest thing in the world for me to unfold the note Dragonfly had sent across to me and read it without Mr. Black seeing me do it, and this is what I read in Dragonfly's crazy handwriting: "Some people have their hair parted on the left side, some have it parted on the right, others have it parted in the middle, and still others have it *de*parted."

Well, it was an old joke, which I'd heard before, but it was the funniest thing I had thought of for a long time. And because I had been sad or mad nearly all morning, when I read that crazy note in Dragonfly's crazy handwriting, I couldn't help but snicker out loud, which I did.

Well, I'm sorry to say, Mr. Black was not only able to *see* all over that one-room schoolroom, but he was able to *hear* all over it too.

All of a sudden he jerked up his bald head and looked right straight toward me and said, "Young man! You may stay in after school tonight!"—which didn't sound very good on account of my dad's wanting me to come home early for some reason.

"Also," Mr. Black said—and his voice was a

little kinder than it had been—"you may lay your book down flat on the desk!"

Then he let the little girl Elfinita, who was one of Circus's smaller sisters, sit down on the recitation bench beside another little girl whose name was Suzanna. And then Mr. Black pushed back his big swivel chair, stood up, looked out over the schoolroom, cleared his throat, and said to all of us, and maybe to me in particular, "Students of the Sugar Creek School, there is only one rule for you to obey. I will write that rule on the blackboard."

He whirled around as though he meant business, looked for and found an eraser, swished it across some arithmetic problems that were there, and, taking a piece of chalk, wrote the rule in big letters that could be seen from every corner of the room, "Behave Yourselves!" Then he laid the chalk down, sat down in his noisy chair, and went on with his class.

But every two or three minutes, it seemed, he would look in my direction, and I knew that I had started off on the wrong foot—in fact, it was Dragonfly's wrong foot I'd started off on. I was wondering if Shorty Long's pop had not only told Mr. Black we were a bunch of roughnecks but also maybe that I was the worst one.

I tucked the note into my pocket when I could, making up my mind that the first chance I had I'd tear it into a thousand pieces and toss it into the big, round Poetry-shaped stove in the center of the room, which was going full blast that morning, making the schoolroom almost too hot for all of us.

But the real trouble came when it was time for my arithmetic class to recite. Mr. Black called us to come to the recitation bench, and all of us boys who were in that group—there were no girls—got up out of our seats and went forward and sat down in front of his desk. There were just three of us in that arithmetic class—Poetry, Circus, and I. Shorty Long was not in the same class I was, and I was glad.

Well, I was still feeling pretty bad and pretty mad and also was trying not to remember the note Dragonfly had sent to me and which was still in my pocket, that note about some men's hair being parted on the left side, some parted on the right, other men's hair being parted in the middle, and still others having it *de*parted.

Maybe I ought to tell you that the very first thing Mr. Black had done when school started that morning was to have each one of us write his name on a blank sheet of paper and hand it in to him. I could tell that he had a good memory and that he would be able to remember who all of us were. Most schoolteachers are very smart.

I guess I didn't realize that I was only half sitting. I'd slid down so far on the bench that I was almost lying on my back, with my feet sticking out in front of me and the heels resting on the edge of the platform. In fact, I had one shoe on top of the other one, thinking about how long my feet looked, and Poetry, who was sitting beside me, had his feet the same way. Each of us knew that the teacher couldn't see our feet because he was on the other side of the desk.

Poetry had the biggest feet of any of the Sugar Creek Gang, as you maybe know. The toe of his top foot was almost three inches higher than the toe of mine, but we were being very careful not to touch the back of the desk because that would scratch it and also because the teacher might hear our feet and know what we were doing.

All of a sudden Mr. Black's big voice said, "Long, sit up!"

In my mind's eye I could see Shorty Long, whose seat was right behind the recitation bench, all slumped in his seat, and I felt good inside that he was getting called down.

I guess I didn't realize that I'd slid down as much as I had because I'd just been thinking about how long Poetry's and my feet were. And since it was arithmetic class, I was dividing by two the three inches Poetry's feet were longer than mine and was thinking that each one of his feet was one and one-half inches longer than mine.

Mr. Black looked as though he was looking right straight at me through those thick-lensed glasses, and he said again, "*Long!* I said *sit up!*"

Well, there was a shuffling noise behind me, and in my mind's eye I could see Shorty Long sitting up as straight as his body could. All of us were sitting very still when, all of a sudden, Mr. Black pushed back his big chair, stood to his feet, swished around the corner of the desk over to where I was, stepped down off the platform, glared down at me, and shouted, "When I tell you to sit up, I mean *sit up!*"

I spoke up quick and said, "Mr.—Mr.—" and then I jerked myself up into a straight position and said, "Honest, Mr. Black, I didn't know you were talking to *me!* I thought you were talking to Shorty Long!"

He glared at me and said, "Isn't your name *William?*"

"Uh—yes," I said, "my name's William, but not W-William *Long*. My name's William Collins!"

And then it dawned on me what had happened. When we had handed in our names that morning on blank pieces of paper, Shorty Long had written his name down as William *Long,* and I had written mine as William *Collins,* and Mr. Black had got our names mixed up. And that's how I happened to get into trouble.

Mr. Black just stood there and looked at me and kept on looking, and all the time I was feeling worse because things were all so mixed up. I guess he was still angry too. Anyway, he didn't seem to be sorry he had made such a terrible mistake. All he said was "The recitation bench is *not* a place for a midmorning nap!"

"Y-yes, sir," I said, as politely as I could. I was trying to remember something my dad had told me, quoting from the Bible. It goes something like this: "A harsh word stirs up anger," which means if you say angry words to people, it'll make *them* mad too. Also, if you say angry words to people, it helps to make you still madder yourself. The way to cool off after a fight is to start using kind words instead of angry ones.

The fierce look in Mr. Black's eyes made me realize I ought to start making up with him right away. He was still glaring at me. Then he folded his arms and stared straight through me, saying, "William Collins, you may hand me that note in your pocket!"

Well, that was too much. All of a sudden I could see the whole world falling upside down, not only for me but for the rest of us. But I remembered about using kind and respectful words, so I said politely, "What note, sir?"

"The one in your pocket. I was going to wait until after school for it, but I'll take it now, since it was passed during school hours and since so many boys had a share in passing it on to you."

Suddenly Big Jim spoke up from the back of the room. "Mr. Black, may I say a word?"

Mr. Black raised his eyes and looked toward the back where Big Jim was sitting. He said, "You may stand up and say it."

I looked around and saw Big Jim standing up straight and tall. His jaw was set as though he was thinking, and he said in a polite but very firm voice, "May I have the note, Mr. Black? I'm the leader of the Sugar Creek Gang. And that's one of our rules—no note writing or passing in school. If you don't mind, the Sugar Creek Gang will discipline William Collins."

It surely sounded funny to hear Big Jim call me "William." And the way I felt, you could have knocked me over with a feather. It certainly was a great idea, if only it would work.

"I'm sorry," Mr. Black said, "but I insist on having the note. You may be seated."

Big Jim didn't be seated. He kept on standing. Then he spoke again, and this is what he said very politely: "In the United States we respect the personal property of others. Isn't that note William Collins's personal property?"

Mr. Black didn't seem to like that. He said to Big Jim, "You sit down," and I saw Big Jim's face turn as white as a new snowdrift. He kept on standing, and Mr. Black kept on standing, and they were glaring at each other the way two angry dogs do when they meet for the first time and each is trying to let the other one know which one of them is going to be the boss. Except that I knew Big Jim didn't want to be anybody's boss. He only wanted what he would call "justice."

Then Big Jim said, "I *will* be seated, Mr. Black. You have a right to tell me that because you are the teacher, but I respectfully repeat, I think that note is William Collins's personal property!"

Big Jim sat down in a dignified way, like a soldier obeying an officer. He sat there with his pencil in his hand, making fierce little jabs on the yellow writing tablet on his desk, and I know he was doing what people call "doo-dling."

I always liked to see what Big Jim's doodling looked like, because he made the most interesting doodles when he was making marks and talking to other people at the same time. He actually drew interesting pictures and didn't know he was doing it.

Mr. Black held out one of his big, pudgy hands toward me and said, "All right, William Collins, I'll take the note. Now!"

Well, what was I to do? Big Jim was the leader of the Sugar Creek Gang, and I had always done what Big Jim told me to. Mr. Black was the teacher of Sugar Creek School, and all of us boys were supposed to obey the teacher. Also, I had my dad's orders to behave myself. And not only that, my parents had taught me that the Bible itself teaches that a Christian ought to obey those who have the rule over him. But the whole question that was mixed up in my red head (which wasn't thinking very clearly that day anyway) was, who *did* have the rule over me—Mr. Black or Big Jim?

I had my hand in my pocket, gripping the note tight. I was wishing I could tear it up with one hand but knew I couldn't. Without knowing I was going to, I turned around quick to Big Jim and said, "What'll I do, Big Jim?"

His face was still white, and I knew that, if he felt the way I did, he was trembling inside and was in the right kind of mood for a good fight. And if it had been another gang instead of Mr. Black that was causing all the trouble, there would probably have been a real old-fashioned rough-and-tumble before noon.

While I was turned around, I could see that the rest of the boys and girls in that one-room school were feeling just as funny on the inside as I was. Some of the girls were crying a little— except for Circus's sister Lucille, who didn't cry easily. Poetry had his big hands doubled up on the desk in front of him. Dragonfly's very small face looked even smaller, and his mussed-up hair looked as though it was trying to stand on end. He had a colored pencil in one hand and, without knowing what he was doing, had its purple point pressed against his two large front teeth. Little Jim sat there holding onto his long, new yellow pencil just the way he does when we're out in the woods and there is danger and he holds onto a stick, which he nearly always carries when we go on hikes. Circus's monkeylike face didn't look mischievous, and I could see the muscles in his jaw moving as if he was almost wishing he could get into a fight with somebody.

Then Big Jim said, "Bill, I think you'd better let Mr. Black have your personal property."

Well, my right hand still held onto that note Dragonfly had written. All of a sudden I realized that it was not only Bill Collins who was in trouble, but it was Dragonfly, the greatest little guy in the gang, except maybe Little Jim.

While I was trying to make up my mind

whether or not to do what Big Jim said, Mr. Black glared down at me with his jaw set and said very firmly, "It's the last time I'm asking you, William Collins! Give it to me *now* or take the consequences!"

Well, I didn't know what the consequences might be, so I pulled my hand out of my pocket and tossed the folded-up note onto the teacher's desk.

And that must have proved to him I *was* a roughneck, for he turned quick as a flash and said, "Stand up, William Collins! Get the note and *hand* it to me," which, for some reason, I did almost right away.

He stood there, the folded note in his hand, behind his big desk and looked out over the schoolroom through his thick-lensed glasses. He said, "Students of Sugar Creek School, the leader of the Sugar Creek Gang is right. This note *was* the personal property of William Collins. However, since it was passed contrary to the rules of this school, it now belongs to me. Also since Roy Gilbert *wrote* the note, I'll ask you to stand up, Roy!" He looked straight over to where Dragonfly was sitting.

I hadn't heard Dragonfly's real name for so long that I hardly knew who Mr. Black meant until I saw Dragonfly jump, shuffle to his feet, and stand looking down at his hands. He was actually shaking, because he knew what I also knew—that the note was making fun of Mr. Black's bald head.

"You may come to the platform, Roy," Mr. Black said, and his face was very set.

"Y-yes, sir," Dragonfly said and started to shuffle down the aisle past the first-grade girls near the front and to the desk.

"You wrote this note, Roy?" Mr. Black asked.

Dragonfly's voice was trembling so badly it was pitiful. "Y-yes, s-sir!" he stuttered, and his voice certainly didn't sound like a roughneck's voice, not nearly as much as Mr. Black's did when he said, "All right, you may read it to the school!"

3

I felt sorry for little Dragonfly as he stood there beside Mr. Black's desk. Different girls in the room were half crying, and all of us were maybe feeling as we'd never felt before in all our lives. We'd never had much trouble in the Sugar Creek School, on account of, as you know, our teachers had all been lady teachers and we had liked them.

All the time I was imagining what Dragonfly would see the very minute he unfolded that note. It would be, "Some men have their hair parted on the left side, some have it parted on the right, some have it parted in the middle, and still others have it *de*parted."

I happened to look at Shorty Long then—and I had to look right across the top of Circus's ordinary-looking sister's head, which had a pretty blue hair ribbon in it. And do you know what? Shorty Long's big face had a funny look. He was looking straight at me, and there was a half sneer on his face, which seemed to say, "Smarty, you guys are going to catch it now. I wish it was you up there, Bill Collins."

Maybe I just imagined that half sneer on his face was saying that, on account of my not liking him a lot. Then I looked at Dragonfly, and he was getting ready to do what Mr. Black had told him to do, and that was to read the note out loud to the whole school!

He unfolded the paper as if it had a snake in it—or maybe the way a girl would have opened it if she was afraid there might be a live mouse wrapped inside.

Then Dragonfly held the paper out toward the window as if he couldn't see very well, blinked his eyes, and started to move over toward the window. At the window he strained his eyes again and rubbed first one of them and then the other. Well, it would have been funny if it *had* been, but it wasn't, although maybe a little bit.

All of a sudden Dragonfly looked up and out the window. Then all of us did, because right that second we heard sleigh bells coming down the road.

Say, if there's anything in all the world that sounds prettier than anything else it's the sound of sleigh bells across the snow! Even while we were having all that trouble, I felt sorry for the people down in Palm Tree Island, where we'd all been just a week before, because they never have any snow or any sleigh bells.

Mr. Black's voice broke into my thoughts like a big finger being poked into a pretty soap bubble. He said, "All right, Gilbert"—meaning Dragonfly—"you may quit stalling! *Read the note!*"

Dragonfly strained his eyes again, swallowed the way a scrawny-necked rooster does when it is trying to swallow something too large for its thin neck. Then he looked at me like a sick chicken, as much as to say, "Well, here goes . . . sink or swim, live or die, survive or perish."

He also reminded me of a boy in swimming, getting ready to duck himself, who takes hold of his nose with one hand, gets ready, shuts his eyes, and plunks himself under.

All the time the sleigh bells were getting closer and closer. They seemed to be coming very fast straight for the schoolhouse. In fact, I looked past Dragonfly's head and saw two frisky, high-stepping horses hitched to a big bobsled swing through the open gate into the lane that runs along the edge of our schoolyard and come dashing, with bells ringing wildly, right toward the woodshed and the big maple tree.

Dragonfly swallowed again and strained his eyes at the note, just as a man's big voice outside called to the horses and said, "Whoa!" which is what you say to horses you are driving when you want them to stop.

Well, we couldn't have heard Dragonfly anyway. Besides, not a one of us wanted to. As I looked out the window, the horses pawed and pranced in a very proud way. Their bells were jingling and jangling, and the man was calling, "Whoa, Blixen! Whoa, there, Donner!" Blixen and Donner, of course, were the names of two of the reindeer in the poem called "The Night Before Christmas."

I looked at Poetry, who always liked that poem so well, and his lips were already moving.

I knew that if we'd been somewhere else and he had had half a chance, he'd have been saying,

> "'Twas the night before Christmas
> When all through the house,
> Not a creature was stirring,
> Not even a mouse."

That's a great poem. I had even memorized it my lazy self. Anyway, those sleigh bells saved Dragonfly's life—or his skin maybe—because Mr. Black said, "Quick, everybody in your seats. We're having company. Act natural. Start studying!"

Well, it was natural for *some* of us to start studying, and for some of us it would have been more natural to *stop* studying. But right that second I heard a woman's musical voice, and something inside me just started ringing like sleigh bells. It made me feel so good I could have shouted out loud, but I didn't dare.

I knew, though, that if I'd been outside I would've, because the musical voice I'd heard was the pretty voice of our pretty other teacher, whom we'd all liked and who had gotten married while we were on our vacation in Palm Tree Island—and shouldn't have. At least she shouldn't have without maybe asking the Sugar Creek Gang what we thought about it.

Suddenly Mr. Black cleared his throat loud enough to be heard above the noise of the jingling sleigh bells and the noise in the schoolroom, such as the shuffling of feet and the closing of books and the sniffling of Dragonfly, who had a cold—Dragonfly nearly always had a cold in the winter and hay fever in the summer and nearly always had one of his dad's big red bandanna handkerchiefs in—and also out of—his pocket.

Just looking at Dragonfly's red bandanna reminded me of what had happened down on Palm Tree Island. For a second I could see Dragonfly down there, sneezing and sneezing and sneezing, and I could see—and *smell*—the big brown billy goat that belonged to Old Man Paddler's lost twin brother.

But my thoughts came back in a flash to our one-room school when I heard our teacher say, "Attention, everybody"—meaning all of us please keep stiller than we were, as he might have something important to say.

He said, "Students of Sugar Creek School, I want all of you to act as if nothing has happened. Now, we've planned a little surprise for you all today—a bobsled ride at the noon hour. *Attention!*" He raised his big voice and lowered his bushy black eyebrows at the same time. "Some of you boys don't deserve this surprise—"

He stopped and looked straight toward where I was sitting, and for some reason I was chewing gum—not even realizing I was doing it—although I knew it was against the rule to chew gum in school.

Anyway, I'd read a lot of advertisements in newspapers and magazines that said chewing gum was good for your nerves. And I really felt nervous that morning, what with getting called down and all the excitement and everything else that was going on, and also all the trouble I'd had at home, and with my dad planning to deal with me that night when I got home from school, and everything. So hardly knowing I was going to do it, I had taken some gum from Circus, who had slipped it to me very quietly just a jiffy before. I had it in my mouth, chewing vigorously.

Mr. Black, with his eyebrows down and his voice up, thundered at me, "William Collins! *Take that gum out of your mouth!*"

Well, it wasn't funny, but almost half the school snickered, even some of the girls. But nobody had time to laugh, on account of Mr. Black's shushing everybody and saying, *"Order!"*

Right away there was a little order.

Then he said, "Lay aside your work!" which most of us did. The rest of us had already laid it aside.

Then he said, "I want absolutely perfect behavior on this sleigh ride. Understand?" He glared at us, and we understood.

Then he said, "Everybody wear your coats and caps and boots and don't act like a pack of animals."

Boy, oh, boy, oh, boy! This was going to be more fun than you could shake a stick at—a bobsled ride with our pretty other teacher and also with her husband. They lived about a mile up the road from the schoolhouse, and he was a farmer whom all of us boys knew and liked, most farmers being very fine people. The only thing was, we had all been kind of mad at him for marrying our teacher. Maybe he was going to try to make up for all the trouble he had caused us by taking us for a ride.

Anyway, we were really going to have fun.

Well, I hadn't any more than got my gum out of my mouth than I heard a sort of rustle beside me, and it was Circus's hand passing something to me. It was a folded piece of paper that looked like the one Dragonfly had had a minute before and was my personal property. So just as quick as I could, I wrapped the gum in that note, smashing it in good and hard, so as to make the gum stick to it and also to make it hard for anybody to ever read what Dragonfly had written.

Then school was dismissed, and there was a sound like a barnyard full of chickens and hogs and cattle and barking dogs as we made a dive for our coats and caps and boots at the back of the schoolroom. The girls went almost as noisily as the boys—my dad says most girls act like boys do anyway until they are a dozen years old. Then some of them start acting like girls, which is just as bad.

But a *bobsled* ride! With a whole gang of laughing, yelling, talking, screaming boys and girls!

4

Going on a bobsled ride with the Sugar Creek Gang and all the rest of Sugar Creek School is almost the most fun a guy can have. In about seven minutes nearly all of us, with coats on, had finished eating our lunch, most of us still chewing the last three bites.

And I never saw a man teacher act as polite as Mr. Black when we were having company. You would have thought all of us had been perfect all morning, the way he talked to Miss Brown, whose name wasn't Miss Brown anymore but was Mrs. Jesperson. That's a Scandinavian name and means she had married a Scandinavian, which *Mr.* Jesperson, her husband, was. We all knew him as Joe. He was a very polite person, and when he talked, it sounded as if he was singing a song that didn't have any tune but only rhythm.

Pretty soon the Sugar Creek School had itself scattered all over the big wagon box, which was filled with oats straw and blankets and lap robes and car rugs. We were all yelling and talking and laughing and saying such things as "Ouch!"; "Hey, move over!"; "Get off my foot!"; "That's my stomach you're walking on!" and things like that, when Mr. Black told us all to keep still a minute, which we did for *half* a minute.

He said to our lady teacher, "I can understand, Miss Brown—I beg your pardon, Mrs. Jesperson—why you liked the pupils of the Sugar Creek School. They are a fine bunch, and I'm sure we'll have a very happy half year together."

Well, it sounded very polite. I looked from where I was sitting beside and behind different members of the gang in the front of the wagon box to see if he really meant it. His voice was *very* polite as he finished.

But for some reason, the words "half year" sounded like an awfully long time before school would be out for the summer and the gang would be free to go galloping up and down Sugar Creek, along the paths, barefoot, and having fun again.

"I'm sure they *are* a fine bunch, as you say, Mr. Black," Miss Brown—I mean, *Mrs. Jesperson* —said. She smiled, but before her smile had finished itself, her brown eyes were looking straight into her Swedish husband's gray-blue ones, and *he* was getting the tail end of her smile instead of Mr. Black.

"I'm sorry I won't be able to go along," Mr. Black said. "I have some work to outline for the seventh grade. Be sure to have everybody back by one thirty."

Poetry, beside me, said, "Hey! He's giving us an extra half hour!" which he was, and which was the first thing I'd noticed about our new teacher that made me think maybe I was going to like him a little bit, even if he *had* scolded me and even if he wasn't a good enough citizen of the United States to respect the personal property of others.

Several times during that ride, I looked up from where I was sitting to our pretty lady other teacher and her husband. I noticed they were looking at each other as if they thought each other was the most important person in the world.

Pretty soon we were off—with the horses prancing, with Mr. and Mrs. Jesperson sitting together at the front, with Mrs. Jesperson helping to drive a little, with the rest of us behind them, and with the sleigh bells jingling and jangling and all of us yelling and hollering and calling to each other and laughing and having a great time.

It was while we were on that bobsled ride that Shorty Long said something that made me not like him even more than I didn't already.

There were all kinds of interesting things to see along the roadside and on the different farms we passed, such as horses and cattle and sheep and hogs and trees, which, with so much snow on them, looked like great white ghosts. Snowdrifts were piled everywhere. *They* looked like a lot of big rocks and little hills with white blankets on them.

Poetry, who was very good in arithmetic, was making up problems all along the way and counting cows and sheep. When we passed Mr.

Jesperson's farm, there were a lot of cows standing very close together in the barnyard. There were so many of them that it looked as if there were maybe a hundred altogether. Our horses were going so fast, and everybody was yelling and talking so loud, that I could hardly hear Poetry say, "Look! There are seventy-nine cows!"

I looked, and we were already passing the big red barn, so I said, "You can't count that fast. They're too close together to count 'em!"

"There were seventy-nine," Poetry said, and he sounded so sure I almost believed him.

Soon we came to another farm, and there were what looked to be maybe a hundred hogs and sheep and cattle, all in the same big barnyard. Poetry nudged me and looked out at the animals and said, "See, Bill, I'm really *good* in arithmetic. There are twenty-seven sheep, thirty-four cows, and fifty-three hogs."

"You *can't* count that fast," I said.

Little Jim piped up and said the same thing, and so did Dragonfly, who was always very poor in arithmetic.

Well, we were coming to another farm where there were a lot of Holstein milk cows out in the barnyard. Holsteins are black-and-white cows, which give lots of milk but with not as much cream on it as the milk of Jersey or Guernsey cows.

There looked to be maybe thirty cows, but as fast and as carefully I counted, I couldn't possibly be sure how many there were.

But Poetry squawked in his ducklike voice, "There are thirty-three Holstein cows, and in the pen beside the silo," he finished, "are forty-one pigs."

"Keep still!" I said to him. "Don't remind me of school. I want to forget it."

Circus looked at me—I was all slouched down on one elbow—and he said, "Hey, Long, sit up!"

And I yelled back at him, for he was sitting up pretty straight against the corner of the other end of the wagon box, "I'll *sit* up if you'll *shut* up!" except that I wouldn't, and I didn't, but I knew Circus was only kidding me.

Soon we would be coming to the Collins farm, and my dad's cows and sheep and horses and hogs would be out there for Poetry to count. It always felt good to get near our house. The great red barn, the old iron pump at the end of the walk not far from the ordinary-looking house, and the big walnut tree close by, where in the summertime the gang had a high swing, the woodshed—just looking at it all gave me a homesick feeling.

But almost right away I didn't feel very happy, because Shorty Long, who was sitting beside Dragonfly and talking Openglopish with him, raised his voice and yelled to me, "Is that where you live, William?"

I didn't want to answer, and I didn't, but somebody else's voice did. Some girl's voice, I think it was, but I couldn't tell whose. She said, "Sure, that's where he lives."

Then Shorty Long yelled out loud enough for everybody to hear and said, "In that funny-looking little red house?" And he pointed toward our red-painted woodshed.

I was boiling inside at him anyway for calling me "William" and for reminding me of Mr. Black, when he said, "Look, girls, there's where William Collins lives—in that little red house. Some boys' fathers keep them in the woodshed so much they actually *live* there."

I knew my face was as red as my hair, and it was just too bad that the distance between Shorty Long and me was too far for one of my already doubled-up fists to reach his jaw.

"Look there!" Poetry said, gesturing toward our farm. "There are three cows, twenty-four pigs, and thirty-eight sheep!"

Well, I happened to know that was exactly right, because I knew how many cows and pigs and sheep we had. But I also knew that Poetry *didn't* know, because Dad had just bought a lot of sheep. So I said to him, "For once you're right. But how can you tell?"

A half dozen others of us all of a sudden spoke up and said, "All right, smart guy, how can you count so fast?"

Then Poetry laughed and straightened up and said, "Fish. You're fish. I knew you would bite on that nice fat worm. It's as easy as pie to tell how many farm animals there are in a field or pasture or barnyard, if you know your arithmetic. You just count all the legs, and divide by four, and you have the answer."

I have to admit that Poetry's joke made me feel like a fish, all right, and I also have to admit that it was funny. "You didn't make that one up yourself," I said to him, and he said, "Nope, I just read it in a magazine!"

And Dragonfly, who hadn't been getting any attention but had spent most of his time on the ride talking to and listening to Shorty Long—both of them talking Openglopish—all of a sudden swished his dad's red bandanna out of his pocket and started sneezing. He actually sneezed six times in a row and said, "Thopis cropazopy opold opoats stropaw! OpI'm opallopergopic topo opit!" which in our language means, "This crazy old oats straw! I'm allergic to it." And it looked as if he was.

Miss Brown—I mean, Mrs. Jesperson—wasn't helping drive just then. She was, in fact, looking at all of us as if she thought we were the finest gang of schoolkids she ever saw (which maybe we were—she'd never taught in any other school). Then she said, "How did you like Palm Tree Island, Roy?"—meaning Dragonfly. "Were you allergic to anything down there?"

"He was allergic to *everything*," Little Jim piped up.

And Shorty Long, trying to say something bright, said, "He was so snobbish, he turned up his nose at everything!" which maybe *was* a little funny but not much.

In a few minutes the horses were going like a house afire down a nice, pretty little hill.

After that we crossed a narrow iron bridge, which spanned a small stream named Wolf Creek. Then we went up a hill on the other side, and all of a sudden we came to a white church at the top of the hill on the left side, which was the church where all the Sugar Creek Gang and most of their parents went every Sunday and also in the middle of the week on prayer meeting night.

Right across the road from the church was another country schoolhouse, which had *two* rooms in it and also had two teachers, and almost three times as many boys and girls went to it as went to our school.

Seeing a lot of boys and girls outside reminded us that it was still the noon hour. The boys and girls were playing in the church-yard, which was almost twice as large as the schoolyard we played in at Sugar Creek School. They had made a big circle and were playing fox and geese in the snow, which is a game we all have a lot of fun playing at our school too.

Seeing the church must have reminded our pretty lady other teacher of some of the short Christian choruses that we used to sing in our school. She was an honest-to-goodness Christian schoolteacher and liked the gospel songs very much and also had a good singing voice. Cheerfully she said, "Let's sing a chorus for the boys and girls out there." She started to sing one that we all liked and which our school used to sing for opening exercises.

As soon as she started it, I looked over at

Shorty Long to see what he would think about it, not knowing whether he believed in songs like that and being almost sure he didn't. He didn't act like the kind of person who would like them. I studied his face to see what he was thinking. Almost all of us were singing noisily, though also a bit bashfully, and also enjoying it, mostly on account of our liking our friendly other teacher so well. We liked the song even better because we liked her. I also liked it better because I thought Shorty Long didn't.

Well, he *really* didn't. He just sat there looking glum and bored and looking around at different ones of us to see if there were any of us who didn't like it either, but all of us did. He also looked as if he felt more important than any of the rest of us, and it seemed he was looking to see if any of us felt as snobbish as he did, and none of us did. So he was the only one who wasn't trying to sing except Dragonfly, who didn't have a good voice and who was what is called a monotone, meaning his tones were all on the same pitch and sounded like a small frog croaking along Sugar Creek in the summertime.

Well, there was something awfully nice about a whole gang of boys and girls singing that chorus the way we used to. One of the reasons we all liked Miss Brown—Mrs. Jesperson, I mean—very much was that she not only claimed to be a Christian but she acted like one. She was sort of like one of the peach trees in my dad's orchard, which was not only a peach tree but actually had big, luscious peaches on it every year. She also understood boys, not getting mad at us if at any time we made a mistake and not always looking for somebody to blame something on.

I stopped singing when I noticed Shorty Long looking disgusted and grumbling to Dragonfly at the same time, and I got my ear close and heard him say, "It's sissified! It sounds like a lot of pigs squealing. Who wants to have a Sunday school all the time!"

Dragonfly got a funny look on his face, which I'd never seen there before, and all of a sudden I had the strangest feeling around my chest. It was a scared kind of feeling, as if maybe Dragonfly was *believing* Shorty Long. I looked at Big Jim's fuzzy mustache and at his face to see what *he* thought, since he was the leader of our gang. And right away I felt better, because he was singing along with all the rest of us, except that he was doing it in a more dignified way on account of being older. I noticed he was watching our minister's daughter, Sylvia, who was the oldest girl in the sled and also maybe the prettiest. She was singing too. I sort of felt that Big Jim liked the song better because she liked it.

Poetry was squawking along beside me in his half-boy's-half-man's voice. Circus's extra sweet voice sounded good. Little Jim's was like the voice of a little musical mouse.

Well, Dragonfly still had that odd look on his face as though he was ashamed of all of us or else couldn't stand to be made fun of by Shorty Long. Right away I knew Shorty was what the Bible calls "tempting" Dragonfly to be ashamed of being a Christian, and also right away I didn't like Shorty Long even worse.

I noticed something else too, and that was that Shorty Long was showing something to Dragonfly secretly, something printed on a piece of paper. He would hold it behind his coat, and then he and Dragonfly would look at it.

Just then Dragonfly looked at me, and he had the strangest look in his eyes. Then both of them started talking Openglopish again, which none of the rest of us knew well enough to understand. I could *talk* it pretty well but couldn't *hear* it half as well, and they were talking it so fast.

I had a feeling that whatever they were talking about wasn't something I would like if I heard it—and then I saw it wasn't only something *printed* they were looking at, but there were also some drawings. I got just a glimpse of them before Shorty Long saw me looking and shoved them inside a brown envelope. It looked as if there was some printing at the bottom of the drawings, which he was reading in Openglopish to Dragonfly.

Dragonfly still had that look on his face as if he was doing something he oughtn't.

Well, there must have been some boys who attended that two-room school who felt as uppish as Shorty Long looked right that minute and who didn't appreciate good music, or else they were just ordinary boys who, the minute they saw anybody going past in the wintertime, wanted to throw snowballs at them. Some of those boys stopped playing and dashed out of their fox-and-geese ring toward the road and started scooping up handfuls of snow and making snowballs and throwing them toward us, which they shouldn't have done because they might hit our horses.

I wanted to have a good old-fashioned snowball fight, and I wished that the horses would stop and we could all jump out and have one.

It looked easy not to get hit. All we had to do was to duck down into the wagon box, and the snowballs would either fly over our heads or hit the sideboard or somewhere, anywhere except hit us. Before I could get down, though, one hard snowball crashed against my shoulder, and our teacher commanded, "Quick! *Down*—all of you—so you won't get hit!"

And every one of us ducked while a whole shower of snowballs went swishing over our heads like a flock of white pigeons flying over our barn.

Then suddenly I felt myself being jerked and jostled, and all of us bumped into each other, and the sleigh bells on the horses started jingling and jangling and acting as if they had gone wild.

And Mr. Jesperson yelled to the horses, "Whoa! Steady, boys!" But his voice didn't do any good. Also I could see him pulling hard on the lines he was driving with.

Our team must have been hit with a half-dozen hard snowballs by some of the boys who couldn't throw straight—or else they had thrown at the horses on purpose.

I began to be excited, not even thinking of being scared at first, when the horses started running down the road as fast as they could. Mr. Jesperson was still holding onto the lines as tight as he could and pulling and calling, "Whoa!"

At the same time, our pretty lady other teacher was holding onto her husband, and the horses were acting terribly scared. In fact, the sleigh bells were making enough noise to scare any horses into running away.

I had seen a runaway once. It was a team hitched to a wagon with nobody in it, running down the road as fast as they could go, looking to be going maybe thirty or forty miles an hour, which is terribly fast for a team of horses and a wagon.

Almost right away we came to a road that turns south and our team decided to turn down that road, and our big sled slid and skidded around the corner terribly fast. Before we had time to get scared any worse, the back of the sled flew around with a grinding noise and swished into a ditch where there was a deep snowdrift.

It is a strange feeling being scared and not having time to think, and not being sure whether you are in danger but knowing you are, and hoping you won't get hurt and wondering if you will, and thinking about your mom and dad and your baby sister, and wondering if you'll get hurt bad enough so you'll be knocked unconscious and won't see anybody for a while. Most of the girls began to scream and scream and scream, as if they were already terribly hurt.

The next thing we knew, that wagon box skidded off its foundation into the ditch and turned upside down with all of us either in it or dumped out of it at the same time.

The *next* thing I knew, I couldn't see anything because I was underneath the wagon box. It was dark. I could hear kids screaming all around me, and I wondered if anybody was badly hurt and hoped nobody was, not even me.

So there we were, many of us under that upside-down wagon and some of us outside in the snowdrifts, and all of us making a lot of noise. I could hear kids screaming all around me, because so many of us were scared almost half to death. I was a little bit scared myself.

5

I guess it was a good thing there was a great big fluffy snowdrift there, because it turned out that hardly a one of us got hurt. Big Jim had a scratch on the back of his hand, which wasn't bad and which Sylvia's mom dressed right away. Our sled had been kind enough to turn upside down almost in front of our minister's house. Sylvia's mom put a little antiseptic on the hand and then tied it up with a bandage.

Sylvia's father came out to help turn the wagon right side up again. In a few minutes a half-dozen neighbor farmers were there and most of the kids from the other school. The men put the wagon box on again. Joe Jesperson had stopped the horses almost right away after the accident, and they hadn't run away as I was afraid they would.

Sylvia's father, who is one of the best ministers we ever had and who preaches all his sermons from the Bible, told us we ought to be thankful, which we were. Also he was the kind of minister who was always looking for a chance to tell people things about the Savior, so he asked everybody to be quiet.

I was glad he was there, because I'll have to admit I was trembling inside, and I knew I must have been more scared than I thought I was. He was not only a very nice human being who liked kids and had laughed when he found out none of us was really hurt, but he said it would be a good time for us to stop and give thanks to the Lord Himself for having spared us all.

And do you know what? Right out there along that roadside with all the farmers there and nearly all the kids from the other school and both their lady teachers there, every single one of us bowed our heads, and Sylvia's father said, "I don't believe it's too cold to ask the men if they will take off their hats while we pray."

I knew he was giving us boys a compliment when he didn't say "the men and boys." He called us all *men*. I took off my brown fur cap, Little Jim took off his small reddish cap, Big Jim took off his gray cap, which had a long black bill that was broken, and Circus swished off his very old blue cap, which didn't have any earmuffs on it but was large enough to be pulled down over his ears. Poetry took off his brown fur cap. Poetry and I liked each other a lot, and whenever we could we bought clothes alike. Dragonfly's cap was already off, and he was knocking the snow out of it and off it, and Little Tom Till, whom I hadn't paid much attention to but who was also a member of the Sugar Creek Gang, had his cap off, and his red hair, which was as red as mine, was all mussed up and powdered with snow.

And there, while the sleigh bells jingled

every time the horses moved a little, Sylvia's father shut his eyes and lifted his kind face up toward the gray sky and prayed.

It was one of the nicest prayers I think I ever heard. About all I can remember of it is, "Dear heavenly Father, we thank You for the boys and the girls of America and of the whole world—boys and girls of every color and country. And right now, especially, for the boys and girls of Sugar Creek. We thank You for having brought us all safely through this accident without anyone being seriously injured. We thank You for having given the Lord Jesus Christ to die upon the cross of Calvary to be the Savior of anybody and everybody who will believe in Him with all their hearts. We pray that if there are any among us here today who are not yet saved, very soon they will open their hearts to the Savior and let Him come in . . ."

Hearing Sylvia's father say that made me want to open my eyes to see if Shorty Long had his eyes shut, the way you are supposed to have them when you are praying. I opened mine and looked quickly over to Shorty Long, and—would you believe it?—his eyes were wide open. He was just staring at the minister as though he thought he was some weird animal or something.

We were ready to go again, all of us in the wagon box, when all of a sudden Shorty Long said, "Hey, wait! I've lost something!"

Before the horses could start, he'd climbed over the side of the sled and was out in the snow, looking around to see if he could find whatever he had lost.

Poetry, who was standing beside me, nudged me in the ribs so hard it almost made me yell, and whispered, *"Sh! I've got it!"*

Well, you can believe me that I kept still. Whatever it was that Poetry had, it made me feel good to know that he had something Shorty Long was looking for.

Shorty kept looking in the ditch and all around in the snow, and different ones of the gang, except for Poetry and me, got out and tried to help him. All the time I was wondering what it was Shorty Long had lost and Poetry had found. Dragonfly, who still had a funny look on his face, also was helping Shorty look for whatever it was.

"Did anybody find anything?" Shorty asked loud enough for us all to hear. "I lost—" And then he stopped whatever he was saying and didn't finish his sentence.

When Shorty Long's back was turned to us, Poetry—who had *his* back turned to Shorty and to everybody else—half opened his coat and showed me the tip of a brown envelope in his pocket.

I had a funny feeling in my mind about that time, wishing I would get a chance to see what Shorty Long had been showing Dragonfly, yet knowing that we couldn't keep it because it was Shorty's personal property. Pretty soon Poetry would have to tell Shorty Long he had it and would give it to him.

All the way back to Sugar Creek School, while we were all having not quite as much fun as we had had before the accident, I had what my dad would have called a "premonition," which means that I had a feeling that the brown envelope that Poetry had in his pocket had a secret in it that was very important.

As I said, every time a new boy moved into our neighborhood, we had to find out two things about him, and he had to find them out also. First, he had to find out right away whether he was going to run the gang or whether he was just going to try to. The other thing that had to be decided was, could he *join* the gang? We had two or three good rules for anybody who could become a member, and one of them was that a boy couldn't be a liar. Another one was that he had to be respectful to his parents, and even if he wasn't a Christian, he couldn't make fun of people who went to church. He was also supposed to go to church, even if his parents didn't go—which lots of parents don't, and should.

As you maybe know, if you've read some of the other stories about the Sugar Creek Gang, about half of us were not Christians at first. Little Jim had nearly all the religion there was in the whole gang, but most of us became Christians. Dragonfly was the last one of us to be saved—except for little red-haired Tom Till, whose father wouldn't believe in God and whose mother had never had a chance in life to be happy, which is maybe one reason Little

Tom Till's big brother, Bob, had turned out to be such a bad boy. It is not easy for a boy to become a Christian unless his father is one too. Most boys do what their dads do—and don't do what their dads *don't*.

Well, I must have had a premonition, because I kept feeling that there was something very important on the inside of that brown envelope.

On the way back to the school, some of us talked to Mrs. Jesperson and said, "We don't like our new teacher. We'd rather have you again!"

She just smiled at us and called us all to attention. And while the horses were trotting along and the sleigh bells were jingling and jangling, she said to us, "Boys and girls of the Sugar Creek school—"

Everything was quiet except for the sound of the sled runners in the snow, and the bells ringing, and Dragonfly's sneezing, which he was doing again on account of his still being allergic to the oats straw in the wagon. Most of the straw got dumped out in the accident, but enough of it was still on our blankets and rugs to make him sneeze.

Then Mrs. Jesperson said, "Mr. Jesperson and I are going to be missionaries, as some of you know. That's the real reason I resigned from teaching. Also, some of you know that we have already finished our missionary training.

"You will be interested to know that our good friend Mr. Seneth Paddler, whom you boys affectionately call 'Old Man Paddler,' has undertaken to support both of us while we are on the mission field."

Mrs. Jesperson waited a minute while a lot of us asked questions, and then just as we were getting close to our school again, she said, "Some of you have said you don't like Mr. Black. But I'm sure you *will* like him just as soon as you get better acquainted with him. Be sure to obey him in everything and be as kind and gentlemanly as possible. I am sure you will have a very happy year together. Remember that he does not know you as I have known you, and at first he may not understand you. Please be loyal to the principles of the Sugar Creek School, which have been yours for years.

"I think it was very generous and thoughtful of Mr. Black to let us have this time together. Also I think it was very courteous and thoughtful and unselfish of him to let me have you all to myself for this farewell visit together."

Just about that time I began to feel a great big lump of something in my throat. I felt very sad that I was not going to get to see her again for a long time, still not being sure I liked Mr. Jesperson very well for marrying her and taking her away from us. Also I felt for a second or two that I *might* get to like Mr. Black a little bit, and I made up my mind that I was going to try to be even a better boy than I was.

Well, I won't take time to tell you right now about how sad we all felt and that some of the girls cried and hugged Mrs. Jesperson. All of the Sugar Creek Gang would have felt bashful if we'd done that, so we just shook hands with her instead.

All of us went back into the schoolhouse, and school started again and lasted until recess without anybody getting into any trouble, and Mr. Black behaved very well for a new teacher.

At recess, which would last for fifteen minutes, we planned to have a gang meeting, which we had in the woodshed, with Shorty Long not being allowed to come inside. Dragonfly wouldn't come in either when he found out we wouldn't let Shorty in. It looked as if for the first time we were going to have trouble in our own gang.

I felt terrible when the gang shut the door and locked it on the inside. I knew that somewhere out in the schoolyard Shorty Long and our Dragonfly were talking Openglopish and maybe talking about us, and it looked as if Shorty Long was going to break up our gang if we didn't do something about it. I still couldn't help but feel that there was something in that brown envelope that would be very important. In fact, it might be so important that it would, whatever it was, cause us a lot of trouble!

6

It was sort of dark in the woodshed with the door shut, on account of there not being any window. All the light there was came in through a crack up near the roof at the other end, just above the top of the big pile of wood that was piled high against the wall.

Big Jim sat down in front of us on a block of wood, and the rest of us sat on a long bench that used to be a recitation bench in the school-house itself. There were also two or three battered desks in the woodshed, some of them with initials carved on the tops by maybe some boy who should have known better. I was looking at one desktop, and it had B.C. on it, which are my initials. I could hardly believe my eyes when I saw it, wondering who had done it, not remembering whether I had done it or not, and sort of remembering maybe I had, but that was a long time ago when I was little and didn't know much better.

Well, Big Jim called the meeting to order and said, while all the rest of us kept quiet, "All right, Poetry, let's have a look at Shorty Long's personal property."

Big Jim's saying that made me remember what had happened that morning in school, and my ears started to burn.

Big Jim took the small brown envelope that Poetry handed him and sat very quiet, looking at the outside. Then with a dignified voice like a judge in a courtroom, Big Jim said to Poetry, "You found this in a snowdrift, is that right?"

"Yes, sir," Poetry said.

"Has anybody seen this before?" was Big Jim's next question, and I said, "Yes, sir, I saw it."

"Where?"

"I saw Shorty Long showing it to Dragonfly while we were in the sled just before we had our wreck."

"Have you seen the *inside* of it?" Big Jim asked.

"Not yet," I said, meaning I wanted to see what was in it right away.

Big Jim sat there with a puzzled face, while we waited for him to decide what he was going to do. At the same time he was doing what boys nearly always try to do when they are sitting on something that isn't very solid or isn't fastened to the floor. He was balancing himself on the standing-up block of wood, like it was a three-legged chair, one chair leg being the block of wood he was half sitting on, the other two legs being his own, which were in front of him.

Big Jim held up the envelope so that the light from the crack in the woodshed behind him would shine on it. Then he shook it, and I could hear it *rattle* like a package of watermelon seeds my mom sometimes buys at a seed store in town in the spring.

Then Big Jim got a sober face and said, using *very* dignified words as though he was talking to dignified people, which he wasn't, "As much as I would like to open this and see what is in it, I cannot do so, because as was decided in school session this morning, personal property is personal property—"

At that remark, Poetry snickered in a very undignified way, but several of us shushed him. He kept still, and Big Jim went on.

"On the other hand," Big Jim said, still talking as though we were dignified people, "if we did not know whose property this was, it would be lawful to open the envelope and examine its contents and—"

Well, for once I was glad that even though Big Jim was talking in a very dignified voice, he wasn't sitting in a dignified way on that block of wood. He was, in fact—maybe without knowing he was doing it—every now and then lifting both feet off the woodshed floor and trying to balance himself on the rather thin block of wood.

Anyway, Poetry, being very mischievous and not being able to help it, all of a sudden let one of his big feet shoot out in front of him and give the block of wood a shove, and there was a scrambling shuffle that ended in Big Jim's being upset and tumbling over in several different directions at the same time and landing in a very undignified sprawl at our feet.

It was actually funny, and we started to laugh—until I saw what had happened. His hands reached out in several different directions at the same time to balance himself, and didn't, and the brown envelope got turned upside down in the shuffle. And right in front of my eyes I saw everything that was in it scattered over the woodshed floor.

There was the personal property of Shorty Long right in front of the eyes of all of us. It was a lot of pictures about the size of small snapshots, and also what looked like a boy's drawing of several persons, which, now that we'd been in the dark awhile and could see better, I could see. And I saw *my* name at the bottom of one of the drawings, and it was spelled "PILL Collins."

Well, I remembered what Shorty Long had called me that morning on the way to school, when he said, "From now on your name is just plain Pill Collins. *Pill,* as in *caterpillar.*"

In seconds, Big Jim had scrambled to his feet and had all those pictures in one hand and the brown envelope in the other—all except that drawing with my name on it, which somehow I had picked up myself and was looking at.

And I tell you that what I saw made me feel hot all over. It made me so mad at Shorty Long —I can't even tell you what the drawing looked like, except that it had a picture of somebody who looked very homely, and my name was under it, and I was carrying a lunch box that was colored with red crayon, and beside me was a very homely girl named Lucille Browne, Circus's sister. And right below my name were some words in quotation marks, which meant I was supposed to be saying them, and they were filthy words, even dirtier than the mud in our barnyard looks in the spring after a hard rain.

Then, beside my picture I saw one that was just as homely, and it had Big Jim's name under it, and beside him was a girl . . .

I didn't get to see what the words were under Big Jim's name because Big Jim took it and looked at it quick, then shoved it and everything else back inside the envelope as though it was something especially dirty and he didn't want to even touch it.

Just that second I heard a snowball go *ker-wham* against the woodshed door, and then another and another and another. And before thinking, I yelled, "Hey, you out there! *Stop* it!" I was out of my place in a fierce hurry. I leaped to the woodshed door, unhooked it, shoved it open, and looked out to see who had dared to attack us.

The very second I opened the door, one of my eyes got pasted shut with a snowball, which, before it struck me, I could see had been thrown by a big lummox of a guy whose name was Shorty Long.

Well, I'd had one fight with him before Christmas, and he had licked me for a while. And we had had another one that very morning on the way to school, and I had licked *him,* so I knew I could do it. And since I was already mad at him and since he had just pasted me *ker-wham* in the face with a snowball, I was still madder, especially on account of what was in the brown envelope.

So I made a dive for the snow with both hands, made a hard snowball real quick, dodging several of his at the same time, and the fight was on. I threw my ball *whizzety-sizzle* toward Shorty Long, who ducked behind the snow fort the gang had made beside the big maple tree that morning before school. My ball hit *ker-thud-wham* against the front of the fort.

"Come on, gang!" I yelled to the guys, who were tumbling out of the door behind me. "Let's wash his face with snow!"

Shorty Long was already interrupting what I was saying, so maybe the gang didn't hear me. He was yelling, "William Collins lives in the woodshed! William Collins lives in the woodshed!"

By then all of us—even Little Jim, who liked to be kind to everybody even when he was angry at them—were on our way past the old iron pump not far from the narrow gate that opened into the schoolyard, straight for Shorty Long's snow fort, which wasn't his fort anyway. We'd made it ourselves.

Before any of us got to the fort, all of us had thrown maybe a half-dozen snowballs apiece, which we had made on the way, and Shorty Long had thrown several at us, one of which had hit me *kersmash-squish*, right in the face.

Also, Dragonfly was scooping up snowballs and throwing them at *us*. Imagine that! One of the members of the Sugar Creek Gang playing traitor and throwing snowballs at the rest of the gang and fighting against us! I could hardly believe my eyes—the one good eye that I had left!

And then another snowball hit me *ker-thud-smash-squish* right on the chin. For a few seconds, I couldn't see straight. But when I saw Shorty Long again, he was holding both hands up to his face and ears. With the Sugar Creek Gang's snowballs pelting him all over, he was running toward the door of the schoolhouse.

"He's going to tell the teacher on you," Dragonfly cried. His voice sounded as if he *wanted* Shorty Long to do that and also wanted Mr. Black to take Shorty Long's part.

Well, I grabbed two or three hard snowballs from behind the fort, snowballs that Shorty and Dragonfly had made and piled up there while we were having our gang meeting in the woodshed. Boy, those balls were *hard.* I could tell that without thinking. I whirled and let them go quick, one, two, three, *bang-sock-wham,* straight toward Shorty Long and the school-house door toward which he was running.

And that's when even more trouble started.

Right that minute, the only door to the schoolhouse burst open, and one of my snow-balls went whizzing in to smash *ker-squash* right in the center of Mr. Black's bald head—he having stooped the moment he opened the door to straighten the doormat.

Imagine that crazy snowball missing Shorty

Long and socking our new teacher right in the center of his bald head.

I felt hot and cold and numb. I stood there, mixed up in my mind, then turned and ran like a scared rabbit straight for the woodshed door and dived in. Before I could shut the door, all the gang except Dragonfly was scrambling in after me.

Panting and gasping for breath and sweating and scared, we slammed the door tight. We stood there with our fists doubled up, trembling and waiting for *anything* to happen. It seemed dark inside again on account of our having been out in the bright light of day for a while.

"*Sh!* Listen!" Poetry said, which we were all doing anyway, but when he said that, we listened harder. And sure enough, we heard the schoolhouse door slam shut. Also we heard steps coming in our direction.

I shoved Poetry aside and looked through a narrow crack in the door right next to the white knob, and it was Mr. Black. He had his big black fur cap on and his black overcoat, which I thought would look pretty with about seven snowballs decorating it like a lot of white stars in the sky above Sugar Creek in the summertime.

Maybe I thought that because I was seeing stars myself on account of Shorty Long's snowballs in my face.

I'd never seen a man's face so set and so mad-looking, I thought. I turned around quick, looked up toward the two-by-six beams that ran across the middle of the shed about three feet above our heads, and wondered if it would do any good to climb up there.

"Sh!" Big Jim said. "Everybody keep still!"

Closer and closer those steps came, straight for the woodshed door, behind which we all, except Dragonfly, were.

"All right, gang," Big Jim ordered us, "everybody against the door! Brace your feet!"

And we obeyed Big Jim.

7

It's a strange feeling being scared and mad and wondering what is going to happen and what if it does.

Crunch, crunch, crunch, faster and faster those big heavy steps of our baldheaded schoolteacher came straight for the woodshed door. All of us were right behind Big Jim and Circus, who were braced against the door so that nobody could get it open.

"Stop grunting!" Big Jim ordered some of us who *were* grunting. We were pushing hard without needing to yet. The door was the kind that opened inside.

"There he is—*sh!*" Circus said. He had his eye on the crack in the door. "Keep still!"

We kept still and waited and listened. I could hear all of us breathing and could hear my heart pounding.

Little Jim had his two small hands up against my brown sweater, with his feet braced behind him. He was probably pale. I felt sorry for him, because he never did like to have any trouble of any kind, and never would fight unless he had to, and was the best Christian in the whole gang. He wasn't a sissy either. He could knock home runs on our ball team. He actually shot a bear one time, which would have killed all of us maybe if he hadn't. And the way he had fought when a tough town gang had tried to lick the Sugar Creek Gang was something great. He had a temper that was better than mine, too, because he didn't let it explode and wasn't always saying things he was sorry for afterward the way some of us were some of the time.

"What's that?" Little Tom Till hissed. "What's he trying to do?"

We were still listening, and then I heard it too. Mr. Black was fumbling at the lock of the door and at the latch. I could hear—and then a funny feeling grabbed me as I heard something go *clickety-click-snap*. It sounded like—and then I knew what it was.

Even before I could say it, Poetry said it for me in his squawky voice. "He's locked the door! We can't get out!"

After Poetry said that, everything was quiet outside except for one thing, and that one thing was heavy crunching footsteps going *away* from the door, past the woodshed, down past the fox-and-goose ring that we had made in the snow in the west end of our big school-yard.

Big Jim unhooked the door, grabbed the white doorknob, turned it, and tried to pull open the door, and couldn't.

"Let *me* try it," I said.

He did, and I did, and the knob would turn, but that was all. We all knew what had happened. Mr. Black had brought the big new

Yale lock, which we always used at night to lock the woodshed door so thieves wouldn't steal the wood, and had locked us in!

And that gives you a stranger feeling than being mad and scared and wondering if you're going to get a licking.

"He's locked us in!" we all said almost at the same time.

And he really had. The only way we could get out now would be to break out, because there wasn't any window in the woodshed. And we didn't dare break out, because that would be damaging school property, and we could have trouble with the law if we did that. So there we were, and what would happen next I didn't know.

"Hey! Gang!" somebody called to all of us. I looked around, and there was Circus, up on the wood that was piled high against the other wall. He was looking through a crack in the direction Mr. Black's crunching steps had gone. You should have seen us all scrambling up over those different kinds of short fireplace logs—oak and ironwood and elm and sycamore and ash and willow and maple and all kinds of wood from the different kinds of trees that grew along Sugar Creek.

Up where Circus was, and where we all were in less than several jiffies, was a larger crack in the woodshed wall, and right away we all were looking through it to see what Circus saw. I could hardly believe my half-swollen eyes, but it was happening just the same. Our new teacher was cutting switches from the drooping branches of the beech tree that grew in the corner of the schoolyard. All of the Sugar Creek Gang and a lot of other people had carved their initials on the bark of that old tree— beech trees are the kind of trees on whose bark you can do that.

Well, in my mind's eye I could see myself getting a switching—maybe right in this woodshed, which was about the same size and kind that my dad used at our house when I was smaller and didn't know better than to do things that made Dad have to give me a licking. I didn't mind my dad switching me once in a while, but I certainly didn't want any new teacher to try it.

Besides, I thought, our nice other teacher shouldn't have gotten married like that while we were all away on our Christmas vacation, without even saying anything about it to any of us or asking us if she could.

In almost no time at all, Mr. Black had two long, wicked-looking switches cut and trimmed and was on his way back.

"Quick," Big Jim ordered. "Everybody down against the door. He'll have to break the door down to get in."

We all braced ourselves against the door, none of us making much noise. Almost right away we heard heavy steps in the snow, and they stopped right outside the woodshed.

My heart was beating faster than ever, and I could almost feel my red hair trying to stand on end under my fur cap, which was beginning to feel too hot. Then I remembered that it wasn't on but was probably out in the snow somewhere.

Our teacher's gruff voice called to somebody, saying, "Will you go and ring the bell, please? It's already past time for school to take up."

I heard somebody answer from somewhere near the school and say, "All right," and it was Shorty Long's voice. Then I heard the bell ring in the belfry of the schoolhouse. And then, in my mind's eye I could see Shorty Long waddling to his seat near the fireplace, and I could see a bunch of girls, including Circus's ordinary sister and different ones, go swishing to the door, making a lot of girlish noise getting to their seats.

Next I heard Mr. Black's voice and at the same time heard a key in the lock. "You may come out now, boys, and get into your seats quick. It's already ten minutes past time for recess to be over. You may all come out—except William Collins."

Big Jim let the door swing open, letting in some blinding sunlight, but none of us moved. Big Jim just stood there with his fists doubled up. Circus stood beside him with his battered old cap on one side of his head, looking very fierce. Red-haired Tom Till stood still, right beside Circus. Little Jim was standing close to Big Jim, and Poetry was in front of me. I was behind all of us. I wasn't hiding, but the whole gang was sort of making me stay back.

"Well?" It was Mr. Black's big gruff voice. His shaggy black eyebrows were almost as long as my dad's reddish-black ones, I thought, and when his face was set like that it looked fierce. I had my eye on the two long angry-looking beech switches that he had in his hand.

Big Jim spoke up then, and I was certainly surprised at the politeness in his voice. He said courteously, "Mr. Black, none of us feel that Bill has done anything seriously wrong."

What? I thought so loud it seemed as if I had spoken the word.

And then the teacher's gruff voice came again, and it said firmly, "You may all pass into the schoolhouse, *except* William Collins. You may pass in *now!*"

My muscles were tense. Not a one of us moved, not even Little Jim.

Well, I don't know what I would have done if *I* had been a man teacher with a gang of boys defying me like that. But I saw the muscles of his square jaw tighten, and I saw his arms move so that one hand was against his hip. He glared at us all and especially at me, I thought. Then he said, "All right, then, it's a switching for every one of you!"

And then I got the surprise of my life. Somebody moved, and the next thing I knew, that same somebody was squeezing through all of us to the front, and it was Little Jim.

He piped up to Mr. Black, "Maybe if you'll give *me* a licking instead of Bill, maybe you'll let all the rest of us go free!"

Before any of us could realize what he was doing, Little Jim was out the door and standing in front of Mr. Black. He had that innocent look on his face that he often gets, sort of like one of the lambs in a Bible storybook that my parents bought for me, where a little lamb is cuddled up in the arms of the Good Shepherd and looking very kind and innocent and not afraid.

Things were tense for a minute. I was waiting for Big Jim to do something or say something, but he didn't. He just stood there. We all just stood there, like a graveyard full of different-sized tombstones. I was even feeling like a cemetery myself.

8

The expression on Little Jim's face made me have the queerest feeling inside. He stood looking up at Mr. Black, both of his little hands at his side, and his blue eyes, which were even bluer than the sky was right that minute, looking so innocent. As I told you before, Little Jim was always saying and thinking things that were printed in the Bible and was always trying to act like a gentleman.

When I saw that lamblike look on his face, all of a sudden I remembered the Bible story about Somebody who had come into the world from heaven, who had never done anything wrong in all His life, and who was accused of having done a lot of wrong things, but hadn't. He'd gone on trial in the middle of the night, and then in the morning had had to carry a big cross out through the wicked city of Jerusalem. And all that time He didn't say anything or complain, and also all the time He was as innocent as a lamb.

The Bible says that "like a sheep that is silent before its shearers"—meaning quiet, not even bleating—"so He did not open His mouth." He didn't say anything but let people nail Him to that cross and hang Him up between heaven and earth. The Bible says that He died there and was the "Lamb of God who takes away the sin of the world."

Sylvia's father, our new minister, says that when He died on the cross He died for every one of us so that every one of us can go free and not have to be punished for our sins.

Knowing Little Jim as well as I did, and knowing that his parents were Christians and studied the Bible a lot, the way parents should—and knowing that Little Jim himself understood how everybody could be saved from their sins just by believing that Jesus died in their place and by trusting in Him—I knew that Little Jim was probably thinking that very same thing. While he was standing there, looking so lamblike at Mr. Black, he was probably thinking about that Bible story.

For a minute, I thought that the Lord Jesus had given Himself to die on the cross for even Shorty Long. The Bible says that He died for *sinners*, and Shorty Long was certainly a pretty bad one. In fact, Bill Collins himself was also.

Anyway, it didn't take me long to think that thought. It went through my mind like a little whirlwind swishes through our backyard, picking up all kinds of leaves and things and then dropping them again as it goes across the road and through the woods toward Sugar Creek. So I dropped all those thoughts almost right away.

But I knew I wasn't going to let Little Jim take any licking for me or for any of us.

Mr. Black stood there looking down at Little Jim as if he couldn't believe his eyes and certainly not his ears. Then he looked at all of us, and his gray eyes seemed not to see any of us, as if he was thinking of something else. First he looked back at Little Jim, then he looked at the long beech switches he had in his right hand. He looked as if he was thinking and trying to make up his mind to take Little Jim up on the proposition and lick him for all of us.

I don't know whether what Little Jim said made him remember the story in the Bible or not, but he got a half-kind look in his eyes and on his face for a minute, as though he couldn't do anything wrong if he was thinking about that story, which maybe nobody could.

Suddenly he looked away toward the maple tree at something lying there in the snow. My eyes followed his to see what he was looking at.

But before I could even tell what it was, he turned and walked over toward it and stooped to pick up something. It was the brown envelope that belonged to Shorty and that had in it those pictures of us, and filthy things about some of the girls in the Sugar Creek School, and some other pictures that only dirty-minded boys would like to see and talk about.

Well sir, the very minute Mr. Black stooped to pick up that brown envelope, I realized that we didn't want him to see it. What kind of boys would he think we were if he saw what was on the inside of that envelope? So without even thinking again, I yelled out, "Hey! That's our personal property! You can't have that!"

I dashed across the snow toward Mr. Black and made a dive for the envelope.

Imagine my saying and doing a thing like that! But I was doing nearly everything wrong all that day, which is what might happen to any boy who gets his day started wrong at home before going to school. That's why parents ought always to try to help a boy start off to school cheerfully in the morning, if they can, which my parents sometimes can't on account of its being partly my fault.

Well, Mr. Black already had the envelope in his hand. Just as I made a dive for it, he turned, and I landed *ker-wham* against his side. I also landed a second later *ker-crumplety-fluff* in a snowdrift right beside him and in front of all the Sugar Creek Gang.

Before I could roll over and sit up and start to stand up again, I heard a lot of swishing footsteps and saw something that looked like a flying boy, only it didn't have wings. It also looked like a boy on a football field, making what is called a flying tackle.

Sure enough, that's what it was, except that this wasn't any football game. The next thing I knew there were seven of us piled in that same big snowdrift, on top of and underneath each other, just as if we *were* in a football game. It was Circus who had made the flying leap at Mr. Black's ankles and bowled him over, and there were fourteen legs and fourteen arms and all of us mixed up in probably the biggest snowdrift in the whole schoolyard.

All of us were tangled up and trying to untangle ourselves at the same time, and I tell you it was a very cold and also a very hot time we were having. There was the sound of grunting and groaning, and Mr. Black was half yelling, "Let me up, you little whippersnappers! Get off my chest! Let go of my leg! Oh— let me loose. O-o-o-oh!"

There was more grunting and groaning, grunting and groaning, from all of us, the grunting coming from the Sugar Creek Gang and both grunting and groaning coming from Mr. Black. I had hold of one of his arms, the one that had the brown envelope in its hand. Poetry was lying across Mr. Black's chest in the snowdrift. Only one of us wasn't in on the wrestling match, and that was Dragonfly, whom I saw standing there looking on with a very puzzled expression on his face.

I don't think boys in a school ought ever to do anything like what we were doing. There wasn't one of us that had planned on doing it, and there wasn't one of us that would have done it if we had thought first. There wasn't one of us that would have been so disrespectful even to a teacher we didn't like. But it was already too late and already being done, and there we were, holding him down and afraid to let him go. We didn't know what to do. We'd probably all get a licking, although the way I felt right that minute, I wasn't going to let anybody give me a licking if I could help it.

I don't know what would have happened if

something else hadn't happened, but it did. I heard the sound of a car horn. As quick as I could, I looked to see who it was, and it was my dad's long green automobile out by the front gate.

Then I heard Dad's great big voice calling across the snowy schoolyard, "Hello, everybody!"

Right away "everybody," which was us—and especially me, Bill Collins—wondered what was going to happen next, and what if it did.

There we were, all of us in a fierce wrestling match with our schoolteacher in a big snow-drift, with our reputation at stake—meaning what if Mr. Black got that envelope of filthy pictures and words in it and thought it was ours and thought we were that kind of tough boys, which we weren't! We just didn't *dare* let him have it. We had to get it away from him, and all of a sudden we did.

Almost before Dad's big voice had finished yelling, "Hello, everybody!" Poetry whispered to me, "Bill, let him go! I've got the envelope!"

I looked as quick as I could and saw Poetry shoving something inside his coat pocket. And right away the fight or whatever it was we were having was over.

Soon we were all untangled from each other, and Mr. Black was shaking out his fur cap, which had come off in the scuffle, and was brushing off his coat and saying in a very pleas-ant voice to my dad, "Mr. Collins! You caught us right in the midst of an old-fashioned snow fight."

My dad was looking at different ones of us —and especially at me and probably at my one not-so-good eye—and listening to all of us panting.

"I suppose you've come to visit school, Mr. Collins?" Mr. Black said. "That's fine. Just come right on in—it's a bit past time for recess to be over, and some of the pupils are already in their seats."

"No, I can't stop now, Mr. Black," Dad said. "Mrs. Collins and I will both come and visit one of these days, though. I just stopped to remind Bill to hurry home right after school."

He turned to me then to finish what he wanted to say. "I'm taking your mother to Brown City. Your cousin Wally has a new baby sister, so Mother's going to help look after the house."

"Will she take Charlotte Ann with her?" I asked, thinking of my pink-cheeked baby sister, the greatest baby sister anybody'd ever had. I was thinking also of my red-haired cousin Wally, and wondering if his new baby sister would have red hair, which mine didn't.

"Sure, she'll take Charlotte Ann," Dad said.

Before Dad had finished what he was saying, he was striding back to the car, half talking over his shoulder as he said one more sentence. "No loitering on the way, now, Bill," which was the same as saying that I sometimes did.

Mr. Black said, "I can release him right now, Mr. Collins, if you need him."

For some reason that sounded to me as if he would be glad to get rid of me, as I was probably causing too much trouble, which was probably the truth. In fact, it looked like I'd been the cause of nearly all the trouble our gang had had all day, and it was all on account of Shorty Long.

I looked at Big Jim's fuzzy-mustached face to see what he thought and also at Little Jim's lamblike face, and neither one of them was telling me *not* to go with my dad. I really wanted to go, because I wanted to see Mom and Charlotte Ann before he drove them to the city.

Besides, if I stayed, I felt sure I'd get a switching from Mr. Black. As soon as Dad was gone, our teacher would probably get over being polite, and trouble would start all over again. So if I left, most of the trouble would be gone. Besides, I certainly didn't want any licking all by myself in that woodshed.

But thinking *that* reminded me that there was also a woodshed at home. If I decided to stay at school, then when I did get home later, my dad would be gone and would probably not get back till away after dark, and by that time it'd be too late to go out to a woodshed, maybe.

And I knew Poetry had the brown envelope safe in his pocket.

Just then Poetry called to Dad and asked, "Can Bill come over to stay at my house tonight?"

My dad stood stock-still, turned around,

and said, "That depends—I'll see what your mother says," he finished, talking to me.

Mr. Black took out his watch and looked at it and said, "You might just as well ride along with your father, William. In fact, I think we'll dismiss early today, this being the first day after vacation and hard to get back into the swing of school anyway."

"All right, then, Bill," Dad called. "Get your lunch box and come on! Your mother's waiting!"

I leaped into action and made a dive for the schoolhouse door. My lunch box was on the long shelf that runs along the back wall of the schoolroom.

Well, when I stepped into that schoolhouse, I could hardly believe what I saw. I looked right down the row of seats past the Poetry-shaped stove, to where my desk was. Most of the books were out of my desk and were piled on the top of it. In fact, somebody was pulling books out of my desk right that very minute, and it was Shorty Long himself, taking the books out one at a time and looking inside each one.

9

I don't suppose I was ever so tangled up in my mind as I was right that minute. After everything that had happened and was still happening and which was yet to happen before that day would be finished, I could hardly blame myself for what I did right then. I yelled to Shorty Long in Openglopish and said, "Shoportopy Lopong! Gopet opout opof mopy dopesk!" which means in English, "Shorty Long! Get out of my desk!"

He jumped as if he had been shot somewhere with a boy's sling, so that maybe without intending to he brushed against the stack of books on my desk. They all went *ker-whamety-flop-bang* on the floor, getting there just before Shorty Long himself did, who stumbled over them trying to get away from my desk, on account of I'd made a quick dive for my desk myself.

Shorty Long got to the floor just before I did, and both of us got into a rough-and-tumble scramble. I hadn't really intended to have another fight with Shorty Long. I'd had all the fights that day that I wanted, but of course what we were doing looked like one.

And then I heard a girl's saucy voice from across the schoolroom somewhere saying, "Bill Collins! Can't you live even one *minute* without getting into a fight?" And I knew it was the voice of Circus's ordinary-looking sister, and for some reason I began to feel even worse than I had already felt for some time anyway.

"I'm not fighting!" I barked at her. And it didn't seem that I was. I was just sort of wrestling with Shorty Long.

All of a sudden we let loose of each other and shuffled to our feet and stood panting and looking at each other, the way two roosters do when they've fought awhile and are resting and looking at each other and getting ready to dive into each other again.

"What'd you take my books out of my desk for?" I said to Shorty Long.

And he said, "It's none of your business. I was looking for something important."

Then Dragonfly piped up from somewhere, "He was looking for something he lost on the sleigh ride."

So that was it! And for some reason I began to lose some of my temper. I said to him, "Oh, well, that's different! Go ahead and look! Only I'd appreciate it if you'd put all my books back in very carefully. Of course, I couldn't ask you to think of asking *permission* to get into my desk. I couldn't ask you to *think* at all. A guy has to have brains to do that!"

And with that not-very-nice remark, which I shouldn't have made, I whirled around, stooped, picked up my books myself and shoved them back into my desk, being only a little less careful than I always was when I put them in.

Then I heard my dad's voice calling from outside saying, "Hurry *up*, Bill!"

I did. There wouldn't have been any fun staying and finishing the fight even if it had been one, with nobody in that schoolroom rooting for me or caring whether I got licked or not.

So I shoved the last book into its place, dodged around the end of the row of seats, and grabbed my lunch box off the long shelf by the door. I opened the door and yelled out to my dad, "Coming!" and was quickly on my way out to our long green car, leaving my troubles behind me.

The only thing was, though, I seemed to have a whole heartful of trouble inside me. I was very sad all the way home.

"Don't you feel happy, Bill?" Dad asked as we were driving along down the lane past one of our neighbor's houses—the only neighbor we had who didn't have any children.

And when he asked me that, I felt a great big lump come into my throat. I blinked and looked out through the frosted window. Not being able to see through it very well on account of the frost, I rolled it down and looked out at the clean snow, the pretty drifts, and the blotches of snow in the fir trees that were like big, clean packs of cotton. And for some reason I didn't feel nearly as clean as the trees. I wished that whatever was hurting on the inside of me would quit so I could talk, but I didn't dare answer Dad because there would be tears in my voice, which I didn't want him to hear. Also, right that minute I saw our house and the red woodshed, and I rolled the frosted window up again just as Dad swung through our gate, which he had left open.

Our car made a wide circle around the drive, rolled past the plum tree, and stopped close to the tank where we watered our horses. White smoke was coming out of the little stovepipe of the oil-burning stove that was down at the bottom of the tank, keeping the water from freezing so our horses and cattle could have drinking water without our having to chop holes in the ice. (Sometimes in the winter it got so cold around Sugar Creek that our big water tank would freeze all the way to the bottom. So we needed that stove.)

Mom opened the kitchen door, looked out, and said, "Hello, Billy Boy," which I didn't like very well, on account of it sounded like I was littler than I was. In fact, I didn't want to be called *Billy* anymore at all but only *Bill*, like other men whose names are "William."

I was already out of the car, so I sort of grunted back to Mom, "Hullo."

And she said, "What's the matter? Aren't you glad your cousin Wally has a new baby sister?"

I wasn't. Actually I didn't know of a thing in the world that could have made me glad right that minute.

"Let's get going on the chores right away," Dad ordered.

I started toward the house, where I nearly always went first when I came home, to get a sandwich—which Mom sometimes let me have because after school I was always as hungry as the wolf that ate up Little Red Riding Hood's grandmother.

"Wait a minute, Bill. The *barn!* We do the chores in the *barn*—not the house!" Dad said.

And because I was feeling pretty sad, all of a sudden I just wanted to scream. Everything I had done or started to do all day had either been wrong or else someone had thought it was. I not only wanted to scream, but I did. I screamed and screamed and screamed.

And Mom said, "What on *earth!*"

And Dad said, "That's a fine way to act when you can't get your own way. See if we let you go again away down to Palm Tree Island by airplane and have a good time. Young man, I'm afraid you're getting to be too indepen-dent. You're—"

Mom's voice cut in as though she thought maybe we ought to change the subject. She asked pleasantly, "How did you like your new teacher today, Bill?"

"I didn't!" I said.

"Well!" she said. "You don't need to take my *head* off!"

Right away I was sorry. I had the best mom in the world and also the best dad, and I didn't believe in talking back to them or being sassy, so now I felt even worse.

"They were having a scuffle in the snow

when I drove up," Dad said to Mom, "and Mr. Black was so jolly."

I wanted to speak up and say, "We were having a *fight!*" but I realized that that would be contradicting my dad, which somehow I didn't want to do.

But I was feeling worse every minute.

"What'll I do first?" I asked him. "Throw down hay for the horses?"

"Nope, gather the eggs first before it gets dark. In fact, you'll have to have the flashlight even now. You can go in the house for that, if you want to."

That meant I could probably get a sandwich while I was there, if Mom had one ready.

For a minute, though, I forgot that I'd come home early, and since Mom nearly always gathered the eggs herself in the wintertime before I came home from school, I said to Dad, "Aren't the eggs gathered yet? I thought Mom always gathered them!" and on account of my not feeling very good, my voice sounded cranky again and disgusted because the eggs weren't already gathered and because I had to gather them myself.

Anyway, I made a dash past the woodshed door and was in such a hurry to get in the house and get the flashlight that I gave my feet only a couple of swipes on the doormat. But I hadn't any more than shoved the door open than Mom yelled to me, "*Bill,* wipe your feet carefully! I've just mopped the kitchen floor!"

I gave my shoes maybe seven swipes apiece,

then swished into the house, shutting the door decently, and went around in different directions looking for Dad's big flashlight.

I finally found it on the dresser in his and Mom's bedroom, and while I was in there I saw my baby sister, Charlotte Ann, sitting up in her crib, which had a Scotch terrier design on it. She had her pretty blackish-reddish curls brushed into a sort of curl on the top of her head. I could see that her face had maybe just been washed. It looked like it had had soap on it. Beside her on the table was a bar of soap in a soap dish. Charlotte Ann had on what Mom called a "combed wool shirt."

Seeing me must have made her want to stand up. She scrambled and grunted her way to her feet, holding onto the bars of her crib and standing up on both pink bare feet. Also right that minute, she decided she wanted to get out of her bed—and I at the same time decided that she ought not to. So I tried to make her sit down again.

Now, beside the soap dish on the table was a bowl filled with warm water, which meant that Mom had been getting her ready to go along on the trip to Brown City to see Cousin Wally's new baby sister.

Well, that bowl of water shouldn't have been there. Anyway, Mom probably shouldn't have waxed the hardwood floor of that bedroom, and there shouldn't have been a rug on it right where I was standing.

Before I could even guess what was going to

happen, it had happened—Charlotte Ann caught hold of the flashlight, which she had decided she wanted, and which was probably the reason she had stood up in the first place, and I was trying to make her let go and make her sit down at the same time.

"Hey, you!" I said. "I've had enough for one day. Do as I tell you, will you! Let go! You've got to learn to take orders if you want to get anywhere in this life! Let go!"

I couldn't just *jerk* the flashlight away from her. That would be rude, and also that would make her cry. I'd tried that once before when I was taking something away from her, and she had set up a howl worse than any two of Circus's pop's big hound dogs make when they've treed a coon.

So I tried to twist the flashlight out of her hand without hurting her, and I didn't know there was wax on the floor under the rug. But there was. *Ker-slippety-swish-swoosh-BUMP*, my feet went in one direction and I in the other. The table was tall and not very wide, and my up-in-the-air feet got tangled up with it. Almost before I hit the floor good and hard, the little table and the soap dish and the bowl of sudsy water did the same thing.

Charlotte Ann screamed, and Mom came hurrying in to find out what all the noise was about and to say "Bill Collins! What on *earth*—" which is what Mom sometimes says when such unearthly things happen.

I can't take time to tell you now what else

happened. I knew my dad had already planned for me to spend some time in the woodshed, and I hoped Mom would understand. I didn't know *what* I would have done if I had been Mom and had worked hard to wax the bedroom floor and then have an awkward boy upset a bowl of sudsy water on it and send the water swishing in every direction there was. And also if at the same time the very pretty bowl went *ker-crash* against the floor and broke into maybe a thousand pieces, which it did.

I certainly expected Mom to make a lot of noise with her voice, the way she sometimes did. Instead I saw her face turn white as if she was terribly afraid or something, and she sort of lifted her hand to her forehead and swayed as though she was dizzy. Then she reached toward the ledge of the window that looks out onto the road and caught herself from falling. And then she staggered over to the edge of the bed and sat down on the very pretty green-and-white chenille spread. She held her hand to her heart, which was probably beating very fast, and said in a very kind voice that had a faraway sound in it, as if she was talking to Somebody else and not to me, "That's another one of the 'all things,' I suppose."

"What?" I said, looking up at her from the floor where I was sitting.

Mom still had a sort of faraway look in her eyes as she answered me. "I promised Him I'd trust Him."

"Promised who *what?*" I asked, glad if she wanted to talk about anything else besides me and feeling absolutely terrible inside—*terrible.*

"I'll tell you later," she said. "You just run along and gather the eggs. I'll have this cleaned up in a little while."

And when I looked at my mom's face, it had the kindest look I had ever seen on it except for maybe that time when I had walked into that same bedroom the day after Charlotte Ann was born and saw her lying there with the new baby beside her. Her face had looked maybe like an angel's face looks, it was so kind.

I scrambled to my feet, feeling very strange inside and liking my mom a lot. I hurried out through the living room and kitchen, not intending to stop to make myself a sandwich. But I saw one lying there on the worktable beside the big water pail, which always stands in the corner near the kitchen door. I knew Mom had made it for me, and I liked her even better.

She was right behind me, getting the mop out of the broom closet, and I heard her humming a song we used to sing in church. It made me feel a little bit sadder, on account of I was sorry I had made such a mess for her to clean up. When I went out the door with the egg basket on my arm and Dad's flashlight in my hand and was on the way past the woodshed, I remembered the words of the song she was humming:

"What a Friend we have in Jesus,
All our sins and griefs to bear;
What a privilege to carry
Everything to God in prayer."

And I began to get a warm feeling inside of me. I was glad I had that kind of a mother. I sort of knew that while she was cleaning up the mess I had accidentally made, she would be humming that song all the way through and also she probably would be thinking of the words. And Mom, being an honest-to-goodness Christian, would probably be doing what the song said, that is, she would be praying.

I don't know why I hadn't thought of it before, but while I was up in our dark haymow, flashing the light into the dark corners where several of our old hens always laid their eggs, Mom's idea seemed to be a very good one. I thought that even a boy ought to get down on his knees somewhere all by himself when he was having different kinds of troubles and pray about them. Once I'd heard our minister say, "Any old coward can mumble along on the Lord's Prayer in church when everybody else is praying too, but it takes a real man to get down by himself and pray to God all alone."

Anyway, suddenly, with everything in the world having gone wrong all day, and with my having lost my temper so many times and having also said a lot of things I shouldn't have, and with my dad not understanding me very well, and with Mom being so kind to me and maybe right that minute on her knees cleaning up my mess, it seemed that I ought to be brave enough to pray.

Besides, that hen's nest was right under the big cross beam that had the crack in it, where a long time ago I put my New Testament while I was waiting for Circus's pop to be saved. I took off my cap as our minister had had us all do along the roadside that day, and I got down on both of my knees in the sweet-smelling alfalfa hay right beside the hen's nest.

It didn't take long to say a few words, but all of a sudden I began to feel very quiet inside and to love my mom and dad a lot. I also loved the One I was talking to, and for some reason I thought maybe it wouldn't be so bad to be punished even if I hadn't done anything wrong on purpose.

While I was on my knees, I heard a noise outside the barn and up near the house. I looked out through a crack but didn't see anything. I just noticed the pretty snowdrifts that were piled along the old rail fence across the road from our house. I looked at the pretty woods without any leaves on the trees, and my thoughts went racing down the old footpath that we boys always raced on in the summer and which led straight for Sugar Creek, and the spring, and along the shore to the old swimming hole where we all had so much fun. On especially hot days when we were dusty and sweaty, it felt good to get nice and cool and clean again. And then I heard myself singing another hymn that my mom liked. It was:

> "Whiter than snow, yes, whiter than snow,
>   Now wash me and I shall be whiter than
>   snow."

I was just starting to pick up two snow-white eggs out of the nest when I heard somebody behind me clearing his throat. I jumped and looked quick.

It was my dad. He had climbed up the haymow ladder and was looking right at me.

I wondered if he had seen me, and I hoped he hadn't, even though I knew he himself prayed sometimes right up in that same haymow. But for some reason I wished he hadn't seen me, if he had.

"Hi, Dad," I said cheerfully, but with my heart pounding fast. I picked up the two eggs with one hand and put them in the basket.

"Hi, Bill," he said back to me. "Want to throw down the hay for the horses—a little of each—clover and alfalfa?"

"Sure," I said. "There were two eggs in this nest today! Do you suppose maybe old Bent Comb laid two in one day?"

Bent Comb was our old white leghorn hen, which laid her eggs up there. Her red comb was very long and hung down so low on the left side that it half hid one of her eyes.

"Nope," he said, "one of those eggs is a glass egg, which I put there this morning just to sort of remind Lady Bent Comb when she comes up that it's a nice nest in which to lay her egg. Then she won't go off and start a new nest somewhere where we'll have to hunt for it."

I put the glass egg back into the nest, set the basket down in a safe place, and reached for the pitchfork to throw down the hay.

Dad said, "I'll take the eggs to the house, Bill. You feed the horses and then come on up to the house as soon as you can. We want to get that woodshed business over as soon as possible."

He took the basket and climbed backwards down the ladder, whistling a tune, and it sounded like the one I'd just been whistling myself.

10

Woodshed business" was a funny way to say it, I thought. But I knew my dad was right and that we had better get it over with as soon as possible. But even though I felt a lot better on the *inside* of me, I knew that pretty soon I wouldn't feel very good on the outside. It didn't feel good either to know that my dad thought I needed to be punished, which maybe I *didn't*. I couldn't tell for sure, because Dad nearly always decided that himself. In fact, I hardly ever felt I needed any punishment.

It took me only a short time to get the hay thrown down for the horses, to put it in their mangers for them to eat, and then to get started on the way up the snow path to the house. Even as slow as I tried to walk, it seemed I was getting there too quick.

I sort of circled around the woodshed, having to wipe extra snow off my boots before I could get into our kitchen door. That took a little more time but not much.

It was while I was sweeping off that snow, using the broom Mom always kept at our back door in the wintertime, that an idea came to me that I'd read somewhere in a story. It wouldn't hurt so much to get spanked, the story said, if I had more *clothes* on. I knew that I had a heavy pair of corduroy pants upstairs in my room. I could go up and put them on if I had time enough—slipping them on under the pants I already had on, and then the licking I'd get pretty soon wouldn't be such a noisy one.

As quietly as I could, I slipped into our kitchen door, realizing right away that Mom and Dad were in the other room somewhere with Charlotte Ann. Maybe Dad was looking at what had happened to the waxed bedroom floor, and maybe he and Mom were talking about *me* and what I had done and a lot of other things I had been doing all day and why.

Anyway, I crept stealthily up our carpeted stairway. Pretty soon I was around the corner of the bannister and in my own room where I took down the wire clothes hanger on which I had actually remembered to hang my corduroy pants the last time I had taken them off.

I had to be very quiet because there was an open register in the floor of our other upstairs room, which was used to let in warm air from the living room downstairs. My pants were only about half on when I thought I heard something. I heard my name, and without realizing I was doing what is called "eavesdropping" and that maybe I shouldn't have done it, I sneaked very quietly into that other room and leaned over the register and listened.

Strange things were going on down in that room. There were my mom and pop, standing together with Mom's pretty gray-brown hair against Dad's right shoulder. He was leaning down to her with his face kind of buried against the top of her head, and I could hear my mom crying a little. I could also hear her saying in a half-muffled voice, "Of *course* I care that it happened. That was such a lovely bowl— the only heirloom from my grandmother I really ever liked—and of *course* I care that my nice waxed floor is all spoiled, but—"

Then Mom stopped talking, and my dad leaned down and kissed her hair and whispered something I couldn't hear and wasn't supposed to anyway. And then Mom went on in a tearful voice that somehow also sounded sort of happy, and this is what she said: "But I promised Him I'd trust Him, and I suppose this is one of the 'all things.'"

"I guess it is, Mother," I heard him say, and then I knew they liked each other a lot.

But I couldn't help wondering what they meant by "all things." Maybe they meant that everything I ever did was wrong or ever would do was *going* to be wrong.

And then I heard Dad say, "But we have to be sure we love Him," and Mom said, "Sometimes I don't think I do—not nearly enough."

"I'm afraid I don't either," Dad said.

Well, it certainly didn't make me feel very good to hear *that*. Didn't my parents love me very much? I could hardly blame them, I thought, and then I heard my dad say something else that made me feel even stranger inside, and that was, "I'd rather take a licking myself than do what I have to do right now."

"What's that?" Mom asked.

And Pop said, "I have to give our boy a switching out in the woodshed. I promised him one this morning, and—"

"Can't we forgive him this time?" Mom interrupted him. "I don't like to have it happen just before I go away for a week. I'd feel terrible."

So would I, I thought, but somehow it seemed maybe I ought not to put on my corduroy pants under my others. So I didn't. Instead, I hung them back on the hanger and started to whistle a little. And it was the same tune my dad had been whistling when he'd started to the house a little while before.

Then a voice called from downstairs, and it was Dad saying, "That you up there, Bill?"

"Yep!" I called back down cheerfully.

"Come on down here a minute." *His* voice didn't sound very cheerful.

In a minute I was down in the living room where Mom and Pop were, and they both turned and looked at me with strange expressions in their eyes that seemed to say, "Well . . ."

"Let's get it over with," I said to Dad, and he and I went into the kitchen and through it to the back door, across the back porch, down the back steps, past the broom I'd use to sweep off the snow from my boots. Then we passed the water tank, where the white smoke was coming out of the stovepipe. I followed along not very far behind Dad, and in a very short time we came to the woodshed. The old door's hinges squeaked worse than I'd ever heard them squeak before.

We went inside. It was a whole lot nicer woodshed than the one we had at school. It wasn't dark inside, even with the door shut, because we had a window on the west side, which was the direction in which there was going to be a very pretty sunset after a while and which I always liked to watch. In fact Dad and Mom and I used to like to watch the sunset together when we all liked each other a lot and when none of us had done anything to make trouble.

But when I saw my dad reach up to the top of a tool cabinet which he had on the wall and take down a couple of old beech switches, I knew we wouldn't get to enjoy any sunset together that evening. I felt the way Mom had said she'd feel—I hated to have such a thing happen just when she was going away. I wanted her to remember me as being a good boy and with all of us liking each other a lot as we nearly always do most of the time at our house.

I could see Dad's face with its big shaggy eyebrows, which hung over his eyes like a grassy ledge along Sugar Creek. I looked especially to see if his teeth were shining under his reddish mustache, and they weren't, so I knew he wasn't smiling.

Then he said to me, "Are you ready?"

I turned sideways toward him and stammered, "Y-yes, s-s-sir!"

"You know you've done a lot of wrong things today?"

I didn't know my grammar well enough to tell whether it was a question or a statement.

I remembered what Mom had said, and, remembering all the things I'd done all day that had gotten me into trouble, I said, "Yes, sir."

Some of them hadn't seemed wrong at the time, but I *had* talked back to my parents, and that is wrong whether you do it on purpose or not. Also, I seemed to remember Little Jim walking out of our woodshed toward Mr. Black today, and he had looked as innocent as a lamb and had seemed he *wanted* to take a licking and let the rest of us go free. So I just stood there, waiting, making up my mind there wouldn't be any noise.

Pop's voice sounded very kind as he said to me, "Have you anything to say in self-defense— whether you're guilty or not guilty?"

And I said, "I don't think I did anything wrong on purpose." When I said that, I really couldn't remember anything I *had* done wrong on purpose, and as I looked up at my dad, it didn't seem right that I was going to get a licking.

He had one of the switches ready. He stopped and looked at it and then at me and said, "Bill Collins, I've never yet caught you telling a lie. I don't believe you ever told me one in your life."

I remembered the story of George Washington, who had cut down a cherry tree once and had told the truth about it. So what Dad said made me feel better.

"You really feel deep down in your heart that you haven't done or said anything wrong?"

And I said, "Not on purpose. But I know I've said things I shouldn't have."

My great big dad just stood there looking down at me, and I could see the muscles of his jaw working as though he was thinking hard. Then I saw him swallow as if something was stuck in his throat and he was having a hard time to get it down.

We both just stood there, neither one of us saying anything.

Then Dad suddenly turned and walked over to the tool cabinet and took out a hatchet, which looked a little bit like the one I'd seen in that picture of George Washington and the cherry tree story. Very carefully, without saying anything, Pop laid those two switches down on a block of wood, and right there in front of my eyes he made one quick sharp stroke with the hatchet, then another and another and another and another, cutting those switches into maybe a dozen pieces.

I don't think I'd ever felt so strange. Dad had used those switches on me a good many times, and his cutting them into little short lengths meant they couldn't ever be used on me again. If he ever gave me a licking he would have to have something new to do it with.

Then he gathered up the pieces and tossed them into the little wooden box with handles on it that we used to put kindling wood in.

I said, "Aren't you going to—to give me a licking?"

He straightened up and looked down at me. His eyes almost looked straight through me, yet they had a faraway expression in them as though he wasn't seeing me at all. I looked right back into his steel-gray blue eyes and kept on looking into them.

Then he spoke with his jaw set tight, and the words sort of came out from between his teeth with his lips hardly moving at all. "Bill Collins, right or wrong, I am going to believe you. Furthermore, as far as I am concerned, this is our last trip to this woodshed. Sooner than your mother and I think, you will be a young man. The days of switchings ought to be over with. I know they have sometimes been necessary in the past, but let's count the past forever past, Bill. Let's burn the switches tonight —and let's never again do anything that will make us have to cut another. Shall we?"

I swallowed something that had gotten into my throat. I felt that my dad was the finest, most wonderful dad in the world, and I made up my mind that he'd never have to cut another switch. But I couldn't say a word.

Then his big hand reached out toward me, and I swished my hand out toward his and grabbed it, and the next thing we knew we were holding onto each other's hands real tight, the way Poetry and I do sometimes when we make a covenant of some kind. I had the greatest dad in all the world.

Dad and I stepped out the door into the weather, and the sun was getting almost low enough to set.

He said, "You can put those sticks in the kitchen stove if you want to."

But I didn't want to. I stopped and looked down at my boots and kicked a little snow off the walk.

And Dad said, "No, I think I'd better do it."

With that he turned and went back into the woodshed and shut the door after him, leaving me there all by myself. I noticed our snow shovel leaning against the side of the woodshed. Also I noticed, without anybody telling me, that there wasn't any path scooped from the side door to the other path I'd made that morning leading out to the front gate and to our mailbox, on which was Dad's name, "Theodore Collins."

I walked under our grape arbor to the other side of the woodshed where the snow shovel was. Dad had left it there when he finished scooping a path out to the chicken house. I was about to take it when I heard his voice inside, and it sounded very strange, as if he was almost crying.

And before I could get the shovel and go away, I heard him say, "And please, God, help me to be a better father to my fine son. Give me the grace to forgive him as You forgive me for Jesus' sake. Make us comrades, make us pals, and yet help me to be a faithful father, firm when I have to be and willing to forgive whenever grace is needed . . ."

I hurried as fast as I could toward where the snow needed to be shoveled. I couldn't see very well, and I actually stumbled over the board-walk that leads from the back door to the iron pitcher pump near the water tank.

It was getting close to supper time, I thought, already hungry—or rather, still hungry, in spite of the sandwich I'd had.

I felt good to know I'd thought of shoveling that walk myself without being told to, and I hurried fast to get started with the job so that Mom wouldn't think of it and tell me to do it.

First, I grabbed the broom from our back steps and went around to the side porch and started in like a house afire, sweeping off the steps. Then I worked my way out to the path I'd shoveled that morning to the mailbox. During the day quite a little new snow had sifted into it, so I swept it clean all the way out to the gate and around to the mailbox.

All the time I was feeling fine, knowing that everything was all right between Dad and me. But I was still a little bothered about Mom. And I couldn't forget that both of them had said they didn't love me as much as they ought, and I made up my mind that I would make them like me if I could.

I kept remembering, too, what she had said about what I'd done being one of the "all things." I decided that whatever she meant, this was one thing I could do that was right.

Pretty soon it would be time to eat supper. I decided to get the snow shoveled and then hurry to the house and, without being told to, wash my hands with soap and start right in setting the table. Also I'd ask if there was anything else I could do.

I was almost done when I heard the wood-shed door open, and I knew Dad had finished whatever he had been doing inside.

Then he called to me and said, "I'll get the milking done, Bill, and we'll have supper right away. You can help your mother as soon as you've finished out there"—telling me to do something I had already thought of. Dad and Mom were always doing that, not knowing that sometimes I thought of doing things myself.

But I didn't even get mad at him. I yelled back, "Okeydoke!" and swished my broom around the gate a little, deciding that he'd meant for me to stop doing what I was doing, that it wasn't very important, and to go help Mom.

I wanted to help her, but I was still both-ered about what I had done, and I hated to go into the house. But I swept off my boots, went in, hurried into the bathroom and washed my hands even better than I sometimes do, and started in setting the table.

I noticed that Mom was very quiet and that her eyes were red around the lids as if she had been crying about something. But she was sort of humming a little tune. I also noticed that our box of kindling wood was already beside the stove, and that the little pieces of the beech switches were there on top.

When I got a chance I went into the other room where Charlotte Ann was on the floor with a stack of alphabet blocks, piling them up and knocking them down.

Then I sort of eased into the bedroom where there had been the big accident, and the floor was already as clean as it could be. I got a surprise when I looked on the wall just above Mom and Dad's bed. There was a brand-new, very pretty wall motto I'd never seen there before, and it had a Bible verse on it. I was just staring at it, remembering something, and wondering at the same time, and thinking, and feeling better inside, when all of a sudden Mom came in and stood beside me.

Neither of us said anything for a minute, then Mom said pleasantly, "Mr. Paddler stopped in today and gave me that. Do you like it?"

"It's pretty," I said, which it was. The words were all in some kind of fancy raised lettering on a beautiful bluish-gray background.

Then Mom said something I will maybe never forget, and it made me like her a lot, even better than I ever had, and this is what she said: "I've decided to make that my life motto. I know it'll help me to keep from worrying about such things as happened this afternoon."

With that she turned and swished out into the other room and through it to the kitchen, just as I heard the back door open and Dad come in, shutting the door after him. Then I heard a cat mewing, and I knew our old black-and-white Mixy had followed him inside and was asking as politely as she could for somebody to please hurry up with her supper.

I stood there looking at the pretty wall motto, which had shining letters on it, and liked it a lot. I didn't understand it, though, until later on at the table, when we were having the blessing just before we ate, as we always do.

Then I looked away from the wall motto and out the window. Somebody was coming up through the woods from Sugar Creek. It looked like a man in old working clothes. He slipped along from one tree to another and from one bush to another, as if he didn't want anybody to see him.

He stopped right behind the big cedar tree on the other side of the rail fence just across the yard. My heart began to beat very fast and excitedly, and I felt inside of me that something was going to happen.

I stood glued to my place, while Charlotte Ann started fussing in the other room. Then the man in the old clothes slipped through the rail fence and glided along the side ditch straight toward our front gate. I wondered if I ought to say, "Hey, Dad! Come here!" but I didn't. Instead I waited, and I saw that man make a beeline straight for our mailbox, open it, and then close it again real quick as if he'd put something inside, which he probably had.

The way the man walked reminded me of

Shorty Long, but it wasn't Shorty. Of course, I couldn't see him very well, because it was darker there by the woods than it was most any other place else right that minute.

I had a feeling that there was something very important that somebody had put into our mailbox, and I started trembling inside, because the man, whoever he was, turned and started off like a flash, running like one of the Circus's pop's hounds runs after a rabbit that jumps up before him when he's nosing around a brush pile or somewhere else along Sugar Creek.

I was about to go and open our front door and run out to the mailbox, but right that second Mom called from the kitchen where we were going to have our supper and said, "All right, Bill, bring Charlotte Ann and come on. Put her in her chair."

I don't know why I decided to keep still and not tell my parents right away what I'd seen. But I got to wondering if maybe there was something in our mailbox that was for me personally and that my parents ought not to see it till after I'd seen it myself. So I decided to wait till after supper; then I'd go dashing out quick. It would be a hard supper to live through, because of my curiosity.

I felt fine, though, as soon as I had Charlotte Ann in my arms and was starting with her to the kitchen, for I heard a stove lid being moved as if somebody had taken it off and put it on again. And when I stepped into the kitchen, I looked into the woodbox, and the pieces of the beech switches were gone. I didn't even look at my dad.

I just felt like a million dollars about everything. Both my parents liked me, and also I had a mystery out in our mailbox waiting for me to solve the minute I had a chance.

Just before we ate, we all sat very quiet a minute. Mom was having a hard time getting Charlotte Ann to keep still long enough for any of us to pray, and also to fold her hands as we were teaching her to do.

Well, as I said, it was while we were having the blessing that I found out what my parents meant about "all things" and also what they had meant when they talked about not loving somebody as much as they knew they ought.

At our house we nearly always took turns praying at the table. Sometimes Pop prayed, sometimes Mom did, and sometimes I did, although I couldn't pray very well yet. I had always said a little poem prayer since I was Small and had just got started to adding words of my own. Anyway it was Mom's turn.

We all bowed our heads, and this is what Mom said: "Dear heavenly Father, we do thank You for Your wonderful love for us all in giving Your Son to die upon the cross for our sins. We do thank You that no matter what happens in life to those of us who love You, 'God causes all things to work together for good to those who love God, to those who are called according to His purpose.'"

My thoughts left Mom's prayer for a minute and swished into the bedroom to where I had spilled all that water and had broken the pretty bowl and had spoiled the rug and the waxed floor. And in my imagination I was reading the new wall motto that Old Man Paddler had given Mom that day and which had on it the same thing she had just said in her prayer. I thought I knew now why she hadn't worried too much about what I'd done.

Then, when my thoughts came back again to what Mom was praying, she was saying, "And help us to love You more and more. We know we do not love You enough—none of us do"—so it was *God* and *not me* that they had been talking about!—"but we *do* love You. Bless us all. Bless our son, Bill, and our blessed baby, Charlotte Ann, whom You have given us to take care of, and bless all the boys of the Sugar Creek Gang. Be with Wally, too, and the new baby. And also bless this food for which we thank You. In Jesus' name. Amen."

It was a great prayer, and I knew that everybody in our family liked everybody else.

It had certainly been a stormy day at our house and at school, maybe the stormiest day we'd ever had, with me being the center of most of it, but it was all over at last—that is, all over except my trip to the mailbox, which I'd take soon.

"May I be excused?" I said to Mom and Dad as soon as I'd eaten a lot of supper, and Dad said, "What for?" and I said, "Oh, I just want to go outdoors for a while. I'll be right back."

"Certainly," Mom said, "but come right back because—"

I finished the sentence for her. "Because we want to get the dishes done before you go. Okeydoke," I said and felt just fine inside.

Out of doors, I made a beeline for the mailbox that had the name "Theodore Collins" on it. Every drop of blood in me was tingling with excitement. And sure enough, right inside that box was an envelope without any stamp on it, and it was addressed to "Mr. William Collins, Sr."

I'd never seen the handwriting before, and I wondered who had written to me and why. Also I wondered what the "Sr." was doing on the end of my name. Anyway, just as people do when they get letters, I decided to open it right away, which I did. And what a crazy letter. It had all kinds of misspelled words and absolutely didn't make sense in some of the things it said.

I started to the house and was reading the letter on the way, when my dad called to me from the porch, "Why don't you walk in the path, Bill?"

I stopped, surprised. I was out in the middle of our yard, walking in snow deeper than my ankles and getting my pants cuffs all filled with snow.

"I've got a letter!" I yelled to him. "A crazy letter from some crazy person."

The handwriting was almost as crazy as Dragonfly's had been that morning when he had written that note about our new teacher's bald head. By the time I had got back onto the path again and had walked in it to our back porch, this is what I had read:

Dear William Collins:

Your son better treat my boy decent or I'll shake the living daylights out of him. It's a pity a family cant move into a nabor-hood without a gang of ruffnecks beating up on his boy. I dont know if you are the ones who took my wife to church last night or not, but somebody did while I was away from home and you cant believe a thing she says about me. You mind your own busi-ness and I'll mind mine. My wife has enuff high and mity ideas without going to some fancy church to get more. If she would obey her husband like the Bible says, it would do her some good to read the Bible, but she don't. Your boy is the worst ruff-neck in the whole Sugar Creek Gang of ruffnecks, so beware.

The letter wasn't signed, and it didn't make sense, because I wasn't married and didn't have a "ruffneck" son. I seemed to know it was written by Shorty Long's dad, but why should he write it to *me?*

But even before I got to the end of the let-ter and to the water tank at the same time, where Dad was waiting for me, I guessed the man had intended to write it to my dad, thinking I was William, Jr., and Dad was William, Sr. which is the way some boys and their fathers are named.

Just then Mom opened the door and called, "Telephone, Bill. It's one of the gang. Hurry up. He says it's something very important!"

On the way into our house with the letter in my hand, I kept wondering if it was Poetry and what if it was and what if he wanted to tell me something about Shorty Long and the very bad things he had said about us on the pictures he had drawn. Also I was wondering if Poetry still wanted me to stay at his house that night and if my parents would let me.

I was just itching to tell him about the letter, and also I could hardly wait to show it to Dad, thinking it was probably intended for him anyway.

If the letter I had was from Shorty Long's dad, which I knew it must be, then it explained a little bit why Shorty himself was such a terrible boy, since many boys are bad because their pops don't train them up in the way they ought to go.

But before I tell you about what Poetry wanted to talk to me about, I'd better get this story finished.

As I said, it was the end of a very stormy day, the stormiest one I'd probably ever had. I won't even have time to tell you anymore about

Mr. Black or about the fire in the schoolhouse—which I had planned to tell about—on account of this story being long enough.

And the way that fire got started was the strangest way you ever saw—with Mr. Black inside, and with the windows shut, and with some of us boys on the roof of the schoolhouse, and with our ladder fallen down, and I not being able to get off the roof without falling or jumping and maybe getting hurt . . .

Well, just as soon as I have a chance, I'll get going on that next story and tell you all about it and also about a lot of other important things that happened to the Sugar Creek Gang that winter.